Ann Summers

Madame B's Secret Surrender

Ann Summers

Madame B's Secret Surrender

EBURY
PRESS

1 3 5 7 9 10 8 6 4 2

Published in 2008 by Ebury Press, an imprint of Ebury Publishing

A Random House Group Company

Text written by Siobhan Kelly © Ebury Press 2008

The Random House Group Limited Reg. No. 954009

Addresses for companies within the Random House Group can be found at
www.randomhouse.co.uk

A CIP catalogue record for this book is available from the British Library

The Random House Group Limited supports The Forest Stewardship
Council (FSC), the leading international forest certification organisation.
All our titles that are printed on Greenpeace approved FSC certified
paper carry the FSC logo. Our paper procurement policy can be found at
www.rbooks.co.uk/environment

Mixed Sources
Product group from well-managed
forests and other controlled sources
www.fsc.org Cert no. TT-COC-2139
© 1996 Forest Stewardship Council

To buy books by your favourite authors and register for offers visit
www.rbooks.co.uk

Typeset by Palimpsest Book Production Limited,
Grangemouth, Stirlingshire

Printed in the UK by
CPI Cox & Wyman, Reading RG1 8EX

ISBN: 9780091926441

Madame B's Secret Surrender

FOREWORD

Welcome to the second Madame B novella. We know you loved her passion-packed short stories, so here's a full-length erotic adventure for those of you who like the pleasure to last even longer . . .

Jacqueline Gold
Ann Summers, CEO

My name is Madame B, and I collect stories about sex. I travel the world, talking to women who aren't afraid to go to the edge of sexuality, and I write their stories down in my little red leather journal, a book that's bursting with sizzling secrets.

Until now, I've published these true confessions as collections of short stories. But then I met Alice, a beautiful actress whose off-screen erotic exploits filled enough pages to turn into a novel. So that's what I did. I hope Alice's story gives you as much pleasure to read as it gave me to write, and that she inspires you to explore your own erotic potential.

With love,

Madame B x

CHAPTER ONE

Alice Daumier was dressing for dinner. It was no mean feat: as she stood naked inside the vast walk-in wardrobe that was the envy of every woman in France, no, Europe, she was hugely spoilt for choice. She fingered a red silk sundress, but decided against it: it was a beach dress and tonight was for simple city chic. What about jeans and a sexy silk vest? Too casual, even for a dinner party at home. And she wanted to show Pierre that she could still dress to impress.

From the kitchen the faint strains of classical music played: Pierre's choice, she couldn't have identified the composer if her life had depended on it. If it was up to her, she'd be playing pop music so loud that the nine-teenth-century windows of her apartment rattled. But the kitchen was Pierre's domain. Outside, the sounds of clinking glasses and the smell of cigarette smoke rose from the cafés and bars of the Latin Quarter. She tiptoed back into the bedroom, hid behind the voile that curtained the tall windows, and looked at life going on in the street beneath her. The newspaper seller directly underneath her apartment was shutting up shop for the day, piling up magazines and preparing to lock them inside his hut for the night. Alice peered at the glossy paper, trying to see if she was on the cover of any of them, but he was too far below.

Her blonde hair, the colour of a field of wheat, hung across her creamy shoulders. It was freshly washed and blow dried into a loose curl, and tickled her skin. She liked the way it felt, and decided to wear a halterneck dress of beige silk that exposed her back and shoulders and would allow her hair to caress her skin all evening. She stepped into the dress, sliding the silk up her slender body. No room for underwear in this slinky little number, thought Alice, smoothing the fabric over her peachy arse and small, pointed breasts. She checked her reflection: a light tan meant she needed to wear no make-up, save for a slick of clear lipgloss and a single coat of mascara. No self-respecting French woman would eat dinner completely ungroomed.

Dressed and ready for dinner, Alice followed the smell of garlic, wine and onions to the kitchen. Not for the first time, she said a silent prayer of thanks for the lifestyle she lived as she made her way through the breathtaking interior of the apartment.

The high ceilings, the whitewashed walls and the

marble and antique oak floors provided the perfect back-drop for an achingly fashionable mix of antique pieces, contemporary *objets d'art* and modern designer furniture. A grand piano dominated the living room. Alice smiled, recollecting the early days of their relationship when Pierre would play while she sang. It had been a long time since their impromptu duets. The corridor that ran along the middle of the apartment was lined with posters promoting some of the eleven films that she and Pierre had made together. It was strange, thought Alice, how quickly one got used to seeing one's own image blown up larger than life.

Pierre was in the kitchen, poring over his beloved cookery books. Piles of ingredients, meticulously meas-ured out, were arranged in little white bowls in the precise order they were going to be added to the dish. They might only have been hosting an informal dinner party for a couple of friends, but Pierre's perfectionist streak would not allow him to serve them anything less than restaurant-grade food.

Alice poured her husband a glass of Merlot for him to drink while he added the onions, peppers and cour-gettes that would form the basis of their ratatouille. He took a sip of the wine and tipped a generous slosh of the dark red liquid into the simmering pan. She was touched by the way his pink tongue protruded slightly from between his lips, always a sign that he was concentrating hard, and planted a soft kiss on his cheek. He was wearing the cologne she had bought him yesterday. Pierre was the cleanest man she had ever known, always clean-shaven, always smelling shower fresh and always immaculately dressed. Pierre had a timeless, smart-casual style which he'd learned from the pages of *Vogue Homme*. This evening he was dressed in a black poloneck jersey with faded blue jeans and red base-ball boots. Alice took a step back and admired her husband objectively. His body was still as solid and firm as the day she had met him, and he still towered over her with a reassuring, masculine bulk. He was Alice's senior by fifteen years, but his sandy-blond hair was still thick and if the grooves that ran from his nose to his lips had deepened a little in the past couple of years, it had only served him well: he could do with a little roughing up, Alice some-times thought.

The crackle of the intercom alerted Alice to the fact that her guests were arriving. She buzzed them in, and they, and all their neighbours, felt the whole building creak and shake as the ancient lift shuddered into action, carrying Delphine and Paul from the ground floor to the fifth in a series of violent jerks. Delphine was a friend from drama school who had realised soon in her first term that she was never going to make it as an actress, so had done the next best thing and become Alice's agent and manager.

She had also, over the course of the past ten years, become Alice's closest friend and confidante. Her husband Paul did something complicated and well paid in a shiny office in Paris's La Defense district, and was not remotely impressed by his friends' stellar careers. Delphine and Paul were dark-haired and olive-skinned and given to passionate rows and even more passionate reunions. They made a refreshing contrast to Alice and Pierre's cool, calm marriage. Alice enjoyed the evenings the four of them spent together more than any other.

The dinner party was a success, the way only dinner parties with old trusted friends can be. Even a taste of fame brings unwanted attention, and Alice had lost count of the times she had been plied with champagne and tricked into talking to journalists at parties. But in this select, intimate gathering, everything was off the record. The conversation flowed as freely as the wine and the laughter. There was the usual low-voltage sexual charge that always filled the air whenever the foursome got together, too: the way that you can flirt when you're with trusted friends and you know that nothing will ever go any further. Although she knew she would never make a move on her best friend's husband, Alice enjoyed the secret knowledge that Paul nursed a crush on her. At one point, she slung an arm over Pierre's shoulder and her slinky dress rode sideways to reveal a breast and a nipple to Paul. Only

Alice noticed his discomfort, and the thought of him struggling to hide his hard-on underneath the dinner table and wrestling with his guilt at his arousal made her nipple firm and erect with a private, wicked excitement.

Delphine and Paul left at 1 a.m., taking the stairs so that the creaking elevator would not wake the building's sleeping residents. Dutifully Alice helped Pierre load the dishwasher and took care to wash their precious crystal glasses by hand. She was tired, she was a little drunk and she wanted to go to bed, but it was Saturday night, and she and Pierre always made love on a Saturday night.

Once he was satisfied that the kitchen was clean, Pierre extended his hand and looked into Alice's eyes. She knew that was her cue to follow him to the bedroom, and let him lead her back down the corridor decorated with her own image and through the large French doors that gave on to their bedroom. Pierre pulled her towards him and kissed her deeply, his tongue gently and tenderly exploring her mouth. He ran a broad hand across her arse, making a murmur of appreciation at her lack of bra or panties. His other hand softly caressed Alice's shoulders and collarbone, smoothing down the silk of her dress so that it clung to her body. Alice felt her nipples stiffen and the first seepings of warmth and wetness between her legs. Taking a step back, she raised her slender arms above her head and tugged at the ribbon that was tied in a bow at the nape of her neck. The two triangles of silk which had covered her body floated away, exposing her breasts and shoulders. Slowly, seductively, Alice let the featherlight dress slide away from her body, caressing her milky skin as it collapsed into a puddle around her ankles. Pierre began his own more hurried disrobing, not taking his eyes off his wife as he tugged off his clothes. She allowed him a few seconds to admire her body and watched as he visibly grew hard in front of her. She smiled: even when she thought she wasn't in the mood for Pierre, she couldn't help but delight in his obvious desire for her.

Naked apart from her jewellery and a pair of diamante slingbacks, Alice smoothed her hair over her shoulders, making sure her hands travelled beyond the blonde tendrils and brushed her breasts. Slowly, deliberately, she walked over to where her husband stood trembling with lust.

As their bodies came together, Alice waited for the thrill of arousal to evolve into uncontrollable passion, but the transformation wasn't happening that night; perhaps it was all the wine. Even when Pierre took her nipple between his teeth and sucked gently, a move that usually made her wild, she felt only gentle and vague desire. But she was wet enough for him to penetrate her and his cock, when he slid it between her legs, was large and hard enough to fill her up. The problem, thought Alice, as Pierre thrust deep inside her, banging the tip of his prick on her cervix and sliding his finger in between their bodies to tickle her clitoris, is that my husband makes love like he cooks. Diligently, methodically, and by the book. And while sometimes, thought Alice, he does make me come, I know in my heart of hearts that tonight is not going to be one of those nights.

After fifteen minutes of perfectly executed moves which lacked the animal passion she craved, Alice faked an orgasm, making all the right noises, squeezing her pussy around his dick in an imitation of the contractions of orgasm and massaging him to his own climax. Her prowess as an actress was not solely confined to her performances before the camera, Alice reflected, as Pierre buried his face in her shoulder and grunted his way to sweet relief. He was asleep within two minutes, obviously deeply satiated.

Alice, on the other hand, was frustrated and confused: nights like this were becoming more and more frequent, with Alice's disappointment providing a marked contrast to Pierre's obvious satisfaction.

Alice heard Pierre's breath deepen into a snore and knew from experience that nothing would awaken him from this deep sleep. She also knew that sleep would not come to her unless she released the tension that was beginning to build in her limbs and her pelvis. With a sigh, she got out of bed. A streetlight shone through the slatted blinds, bathing the room in bands of light. Alice could make out the contours of her body in the full-length mirror at the foot of her bed, zebra stripes of light and shade decorating her skin. Stretching her arms above her head and sticking her arse out, she had to admit that she could see what it was about her that drove Pierre so wild. Slender without being scrawny, pale without being pallid, Alice was blessed with the kind of alabaster skin that never blotches and never seemed to age. Although she was twenty-six, her tits were as pert as they had been when she was fourteen. The soft rosy nipples still pointed proudly whenever she was excited.

And despite Pierre's best efforts, Alice was still excited. She ran her manicured left hand, heavy with the weight of her diamond wedding ring, over her breasts, down past her navel, until she reached the soft down of her pubic hair. Her bush was neatly waxed into a soft, pale blonde goatee and sat on top of a pair of fat, juicy labia. As Alice used her forefingers to part her pussy lips and gently stroked her clitoris, she let her mind wander to another man who had praised every inch of her body with his words, with his tongue and with his hands, a man who had once used her body as a blank canvas for the pearly decorations of his cum, who had loved her flaxen bush and the pale pink shell of her pussy. Another man, another life . . . Alice parted her legs wider so that her feet splayed out, as though about to attempt a yoga pose. She could see her moist pussy glistening by the streetlamp's dappled light, and the musky smell of her own arousal filled her nostrils, increasing her excitement.

She slid her middle finger inside her pussy and used her own juices to lubricate the fingers that were working at her clitoris. She rubbed furiously, building up a steady rhythm and rocking to and fro as the orgasm built up within her body. She heard the floorboards squeaking beneath her rocking feet but knew that Pierre would remain asleep. As her orgasm grew nearer, she barely cared whether he awoke or not. All that mattered was unleashing this hot bubbling tide of sexual energy that had been brewing in her since the beginning of the evening; the energy that Pierre had failed to tap into. She remembered the way Paul had looked at her exposed breast earlier that evening, and imagined him comparing her own small breasts with Delphine's round, full tits. Disloyalty to her friend was eclipsed by excitement, and with her right hand, Alice feverishly felt for that breast and tugged hard at the nipple. She licked her fingers, slid them over the erect bud and imagined that they were Paul's lips, clamped and sucking on the tit. This image was all she needed to tip her over the edge into a wonderful orgasm that made the fine hairs on the back of her neck stand up and made her clit so swollen and sensitive that she had to whip her hand away.

After masturbating, Alice often felt thirsty or hungry.

Her pussy lips still so swollen that she had to walk with her legs splayed, like a rider without a horse, Alice made her way to the kitchen. She opened the fridge, pulled out a green bottle of sparkling mineral water and drank greedily, letting the icy liquid spill down between her breasts, over her belly, and between her legs. The bubbles bursting on her skin were invigorating and cooled her hot flesh.

In the bathroom, Alice removed what little make-up remained on her face. She was aware that without the camouflage of her mascara she looked far younger than her years, and was reminded of the girl she used to be. As ever, the last thing Alice did before slipping between the sheets and wrapping her arms around her sleeping husband was to remove her jewellery. Slowly she unhooked the 12-carat diamonds that hung from her ear lobes and placed them on the bedside table. Finally she removed the heavy rings which she wore on her left finger every day, bands decorated with glinting precious metal and shimmering priceless stones.

The expensive wedding and engagement rings sparkled even in the dark and were the last things Alice saw before she closed her eyes and went to sleep, dreaming of a prison made of gold and diamonds, and a man with Mediterranean-blue eyes who came to liberate her from it.

CHAPTER TWO

The waiter who refreshed Alice's glass was just the kind of young man she found captivating: barely in his twenties, dark and dirty and dishevelled despite the smart white and gold of his uniform blazer. She smiled at him as he poured the champagne and watched his high, round arse in tight black trousers as he walked away from their table.

'So we've got an offer for a contract to advertise this new shampoo,' Delphine was saying. 'The money's great, but the really good news is that you'll be on television in England and America as well as in France.'

'Mmm,' said Alice vaguely.

'Are you even listening to me?' said Delphine, piqued. 'I take you out to lunch and tell you I'm going to make you even richer than you already are, and you're not even listening to me.'

Alice snapped back into the real world. 'I'm sorry, darling,' she said to her friend. 'I'm feeling a bit odd today. I get the feeling someone's watching me. Staring at me.'

'You're Alice Daumier,' laughed Delphine. 'Someone stares at you every time you leave the house.'

Alice smiled, but that wasn't what she had meant. Lately, she'd had a feeling that someone was close to her, watching from the shadows. She'd felt it that morning on the short walk from her apartment to the restaurant where she was now consuming overpriced champagne and oysters with Delphine. She wished that the place did not have such huge plate-glass windows and that the maitre d' had not sat them so near to them.

'I know, I'm being silly,' she said to Delphine, squeezing a lemon over her plate. 'Ignore me.'

But Alice couldn't ignore the feeling. Of course, she was used to people staring at her wherever she went. That wasn't what she meant. The usual kind of staring was bold and unabashed. If you're in the public eye people think that they can stare at you in a rude, bold way. And that you won't mind. And that you won't even notice! No, Alice felt that she was being watched in a very different way but it was nothing she could explain. If she had believed in having a sixth sense then that's how she would have described it. She often felt that there was a pair of eyes on her in the strangest places, when she was buying her groceries, jogging along the Left Bank, having her hair done, walking with Pierre. Sometimes, even standing at the window of her own apartment she felt hidden eyes were devouring her. There was something sexual about it, she was certain of that. This voyeur, this stalker, whoever he was, was reawakening feelings that had lain dormant in Alice for nearly a decade.

She was half-expecting to feel the invisible eyes burning her back on her walk home, but she sensed no one apart from one paparazzo whom she knew and was on friendly terms with. She let him take her picture outside her apartment, told him which designer she was wearing, and closed the door behind her. Alice took the stairs, two at a time – she never took the lift and it showed in the tightness of her butt and the shapeliness of her calves.

She let herself in through the front door, called out Pierre's name and got no reply. Good – she had the apartment to herself. The clickety-clack of Alice's high heels on the marble floor of the entrance hall picked out a little rhythm that echoed off the high ceilings. She walked through the living room trailing her hand along the bookshelf of dusty paperbacks, wondering which to read this afternoon as she curled up in her favourite window seat. It was one of Alice's chief pleasures in life to sit in her window seat with a good cup of coffee, reading classic French literature and occasionally glancing up at the life happening on the street down below. Alice's finger settled on *La Chamade* by Françoise Sagan, a book she had first read at school. It reminded her of lost innocence: hers, not the heroine's. Yes, she decided. She would bathe, then wrap herself in her favourite silk robe, and settle in for an afternoon's reading. If she read at four o'clock she would get the full beam of the afternoon sun pleasantly warming her skin and illuminating the pages of the book.

But first, a bath. Alice's baths were legendary among her family and friends. In his wedding speech Pierre had joked that he had begged Alice not to take a bath on the morning of the ceremony for fear that she would become so engrossed in her steamy sanctum that she would quite forget that she had somewhere else important to be. To Alice, bathing was a sensual pleasure that came third only to food and sex. Or should that be sex, then food? She opened her bathroom cabinet, wondering which of the expensive potions to pour into the water that gushed from the spotted gold tap. The old-fashioned tub was mounted in the middle of the bathroom, and the ancient plumbing made a deafening clanking sound. She often masturbated in here with the tap running, fingers flicking hard and fast over her clit, skilfully bringing herself off in less than the time it took to run the bath and safe in the knowledge that the rushing water and noisy plumbing would drown out her moans of pleasure. Sometimes, when she was really horny, she would lie down in the bath, her legs hooked over the side, pussy spread directly underneath the tap so that the jets of water cascaded on to her clit, washed over her pussy and arsehole and massaged her to orgasm.

But not today. Today Alice just wanted to soak her aching muscles and ease the feet that had negotiated Paris's unforgiving cobbled streets in three-inch stilettos. She sank into the scalding water, letting it turn her creamy white skin a vivid pink. A white mist filled the tiny bathroom. Clouds of lavender-scented steam obscured everything, the mirrors, the fixtures and fittings, so that Alice could barely see her hand in front of her face. She lay in the bath until the water was lukewarm and her fingers and toes were pruned and wrinkled. When she could finally bring herself to rise, she massaged an expensive body lotion into every inch of her skin: it was made from crushed pearls and cost hundreds of euros for a small glass jar. She enjoyed the feeling of her own fingers pummelling her flesh, smoothing her skin until it felt like silk.

As she left the bathroom, something underneath the front door caught her eye: a small, pale blue, square envelope. Alice was intrigued. The letter must have been delivered by hand. Occasionally fans found out where she lived and thrust notes into the hands of her long-suffering neighbours, but it was not the custom to bring the letter to her front door; usually, they would simply save it and slip it in with the next post.

She picked the envelope up and turned it over, and almost screamed. There was just one word, 'Alice', written on the envelope but the handwriting told her that this was no letter from a crazed fan. It was far more thrilling and dangerous than that. She had not seen her name written in this hand – an elegant, flamboyant looped script that she would have recognised anywhere – for eight years. Her hand shook as memories came flooding back. The towel wrapped around her body fell to the floor. Alice leaned against the wall, grateful for the cool plaster against her skin. She felt sick and dizzy, as though she would actually fall over or faint without the wall's support.

Thank God Pierre was out. Alice needed to be alone to read this letter. She looked at the envelope as though she were afraid it might attack her physically. She savoured this moment, knowing that whatever the letter said it was going to change her life. She looked around the pristine apartment as though it were about to vanish, and said to herself, enjoy the last few moments of calm; you might be about to lose all this. Alice went to the fridge where she poured herself a glass of cool crisp white wine with hands that fluttered uncontrollably, like a pair of birds in a cage. Only after a glass and a half did she feel ready to read the letter. She tore it open.

Darling Alice,

Of course I've been watching. Did you think that I wouldn't come after you? I have watched your star rise for the last eight years. Sometimes I see you on screen. Sometimes I see you in a magazine. Sometimes I have been so close that if you had turned around you would have looked into my eyes. I have never touched you, although I could have done. I know that you have felt my presence.

I'm getting closer. It's nearly time for us to meet again. And when we do, this perfect life you have made for yourself – a life without me in it – will change for ever.

There was no signature, of course. There didn't need to be. Alice let her eyes fall closed. A series of vivid scenes came back to her in a sequence of highly arousing flashbacks. Bodies which came together time after time after time, a mouth on her breast, her tongue on his balls, hands on backs, fingers tearing at hair and legs entwined and a hard dick which had filled her up inside. And then there were other memories, more bodies, new mouths, a confusing tangle of flesh and a feeling of finally knowing what it was like to be alive, really alive . . . It was like watching the edited highlights, a montage of scenes from films she had starred in. But this was no film. This was real life. Another life. A long time ago. But still, Alice's life.

She had always known that Jacques would catch up with her one day. Now that she saw the letter she realised she had been, on some level, waiting to hear from him all this time. Alice folded up the letter into a tiny square and put it in her lingerie drawer.

Pierre came home an hour later and from somewhere Alice found the strength to behave as though nothing out of the ordinary had happened. She managed to make small talk with him over their supper, but all the while her mind was racing and a pulse was hammering between her legs.

CHAPTER THREE

Alice was eighteen when she met him. A baby, really. Fresh faced, and as innocent on the inside as she looked on the outside. She inherited her peaches-and-cream complexion and fair hair from her father, the London banker James Hill, but her mother, a glamorous Parisian called Veronique, had made sure that she had all the poise and grace of a French woman. Veronique had been a model in her own teens and was determined that Alice should follow her into the world of fashion. But Alice didn't care about modelling. All her life she had wanted to act, and while the other girls in her class were experimenting with boys and sex and drugs and night-clubs, Alice was attending drama workshops, reading the great playwrights and working as an usherette in the evenings, just to be near to the stage and to theatre people.

She had had one or two casual boyfriends and had been on a string of dates but had never gone further than a few not-very-passionate kisses goodnight. Alice had enjoyed the kisses, although not as much as her male companions, whose erections – mysterious hard flesh that she didn't understand – would press into her thigh. But she had never felt any compulsion to take them further, or to give into her admirers' pleas for something more.

Alice's dedication had paid off – she won a scholarship to study drama at the University of Paris. Veronique was pleased because she was bound to be 'discovered' there, her father insisting that she would be able to transfer to complete a degree in a 'proper' subject when her year-long course was over.

There was a gap of two months to fill between finishing school in northern France and taking up her post in Paris. Both her parents decided that Alice should travel to the south of France and spend the summer waitressing. They were keen that their daughter should gain some experience of life outside the family home as well as building up some savings for when she went to university. Veronique suggested Cannes for its heady mix of cosmopolitan nightlife.

'If you make it as an actress, you will end up there anyway for the film festival,' she informed Alice. 'And it won't do you any harm to be surrounded by rich people giving generous tips. I'm sure you'll infiltrate the smart set in no time. You will write to me with news of parties on yachts, I am sure of it.' Alice sometimes wondered if Veronique was not trying to live vicariously through her.

She could only agree that it would be good for her to experience life away from home. After all, an actress needs to have as broad a range of experiences as possible if she is to be a success.

The reality had not quite measured up to Veronique's fantasy or Alice's expectations. Instead of a glitzy job serving cocktails to millionaire playboys on the seafront hotel, Alice's employment agency had found her a waitressing job in a rundown café in one of the less glamorous districts, miles from the sea. She was surrounded not by money, power and beauty but by local workers, the odd travelling student who never tipped, and old men and women whose ability to make one beer or coffee last for three and a half hours never failed to amaze Alice. Her accommodation was a dingy basement flat with a shared bathroom that was so dirty it was impossible to believe you could ever get clean in it. When the windows were closed the heat was oppressive and Alice felt that she couldn't breathe. When the windows were open the smell of stale fried onions and garlic drifted in from the neighbouring restaurant and permeated her hair, her clothes and her skin. On her first evening in Cannes, she decided to knock on the neighbours' doors to introduce herself. The room opposite her own had been opened by a fat little man in a stained vest with an angry face who had sworn violently at her before slamming the door in her face. After that, Alice had decided that she was better off not getting to know her neighbours. Better to be friendless than surrounded by such awful, ugly people.

Alice had spent three miserable weeks in Cannes, and was about to call her mother to say that it had all been a terrible mistake and could she come home when the man who was to change her life walked into the café. Dressed in a tattered white shirt and holey jeans, with a string of wooden beads around his neck and dark, thick, wavy hair that had not seen a barber for months, Alice immediately categorised him as a poor student. Without making eye contact, he took a seat at a wonky table and ordered a beer.

'I'll make it icy cold for you,' she said with a smile. 'You look so hot.' She expected him to smile back at her, but when his eyes met hers their gaze was intense and deadly serious. His eyes were cornflower blue, dramatic in his deeply tanned face, and his lips were pink and soft. Something about him made Alice blush. She had been shy around boys before, but never quite like this; within a few seconds her body began to change in a way that was entirely new to her. The pulse that began to hammer in her throat and travelled down her body like a streak of lightning before focusing itself between her legs was unprecedented and terrified her. Alice poured the beer with shaking hands, noticing as she tilted the glass under the tap that her nipples were as erect and pointed as though it had been a winter's day and not 40 degrees in the shade. She turned her back to him and smoothed her hands over her breasts, both wanting and not wanting him to see what was happening to her.

She had a sudden, unbelievably vivid, mental picture of the two of them naked, his full red mouth wrapped entirely around one of her small white breasts, sucking it greedily, teasing her nipple until it was swollen and harder than it had ever been before. The sudden flow of warm wetness that seeped into her panties took her by complete surprise. Alice had never done any of the things that she was picturing with a man before. She had never even been naked with a man. Until she had met this stranger, she had had no desire to be. Now, it was all she could think about.

She set the beer down in front of him. He didn't drink it at first but held it to his forehead, which was beaded with sweat. He closed his eyes, allowing Alice to look at him without the fear that he would turn that disquieting stare on her again. She noticed his broad, dark brow, framing eyes with lashes which Alice herself would have been jealous of. The hair at the nape of his neck was damp and curled. The forearms exposed by his rolled-up shirt sleeves were lean but muscular, with veins that ran from his fingers to his elbows, and his tan was not the even bronze of the born Mediterranean but a dappled, ruddy brown. Alice wondered if his skin was the same colour all over.

Like the old people who eked out a day's stay in the café over a single espresso, this guy made his beer last for an hour. Alice hovered behind the counter, watching his lips part with every sip. She could not take her eyes off him. From his jacket pocket, he produced a battered old paperback which he proceeded to read, occasionally pausing to look up and stare across the road. Sometimes he would make notes in the margin with a pencil. Once or twice he licked his fingers to help him turn the page. The sight of his long pink tongue and even, ice-white teeth were startling in the middle of that weathered face and triggered a fresh flow of explicit images in Alice's mind's eye.

The mysterious stranger ordered another cold beer, and later a glass of water. Then another glass of water. The nearer Alice got to his table, the faster her pulse raced and the more intense the sensation between her legs became. To her astonishment and something approaching shame, she could actually smell her own pounding, aching wet pussy. And something about him told her that he could too. He was watching her when her back was turned. She felt the strength of his gaze on her bare arms and legs

31

as physically as though it were direct skin-on-skin contact, although she couldn't explain how she knew he was looking at her.

At eight o'clock, when the sun began to set and the street was cast in shadow, he lit a cigarette. Alice lifted up her nose and breathed in the smoke as though she were inhaling the very essence of him. At nine o'clock, he raised his left hand and mimed a signature in mid-air. As Alice wrote out the bill, she was at a complete loss as to what to do. If he left he might never come back and perhaps she would never have this wonderful feeling again. Then again, it wasn't a comfortable feeling. She felt like she was astride a rollercoaster or a runaway train that she could not control. If this is what it's like to be really turned on, she thought, I don't know how people cope. I'm a mess. Perhaps I am better off if I don't ever see him again.

She brought the bill to him and set it down on a plate on the tablecloth in front of him, all the while her heart pounding so loudly she was sure he could hear it. He grabbed hold of Alice's slender white wrist with a dry, leathery, tanned hand. He might as well have administered an electric shock directly to her skin. Alice felt a surge of sexual arousal stronger than anything else she had ever known. Her breath began to come in short rasps, and she was aware of her erect nipples rising and falling as her breasts heaved.

'A beautiful woman like you and an artistic man like me shouldn't have to spend their time in a dump like this,' he said, his blue eyes twinkling. It was the longest sentence he had uttered all day. She allowed herself a shy smile. If Alice had heard that chat-up line from one of the boys in her school, or any of the other customers at the café, or any other man on the planet, she would have laughed and turned on her heel. But there was something about this guy that made even clichés sound resonant, sexy and urgent. What could she possibly say that would make him see how thrilled she was at the touch of his hand on her skin, at his voice and his eyes and the fact that he thought she was beautiful?

'That will be 150 francs, please.' Alice cringed at her own gauche choice of phrase. But he tightened his grip on her wrist. With his free hand, he reached into his jeans pocket – what's in there, thought Alice, what lies beneath that faded denim? – and pulled out a tatty brown leather pouch. He tipped a pile of coins on to the tablecloth and began to sort through them with one hand. Alice noticed two things at once; that his fingers were long, brown, strong and healthy but slightly dirty, and that he was at least as poor as she was. Both these things made him seem less intimidating. When he had counted out his change, he made the coins into a little pile. Instead of putting them onto the plate with the bill, he twisted Alice's arm around so that her palm faced him, and pressed the coins into her hand. One by one, he curled her fingers around the money, making a fist of her hand and covering it with his own. He looked up at her, unblinking and deadly serious.

'I am afraid I do not have the money to give you the generous tip you deserve,' he said. His hand tightened around her. Alice was about to protest: he was beginning to hurt her and she could feel a throbbing in her hand where he was cutting off the blood supply. It mirrored the throbbing between her legs. 'You see, I don't have much money. And with the money I do have, I need to take you out to dinner tonight.'

Alice felt she might faint with happiness and apprehension. Her voice let her down again and all she could do was nod.

'I will come back here to pick you up at ten o'clock,' he said. It was a command, not a question. Alice did a series of calculations. That just about gave her enough time to go home, change out of her work clothes, shower and slip on a simple summer dress. She nodded her consent.

'What is your name?'

This time Alice found her voice. 'I'm Alice,' she said.

'We need to know each other, Alice.' Again there was no room for argument. 'My name's Jacques.' His grip on her tightened even harder. Alice felt the beginning of pins and needles in her fingers and the little pile of coins in her fist grew warm and damp with her sweat. Then he let her go, and pushed her away, leaving her with a somersaulting stomach, numb hand and a clit which seemed to beat between her legs like a tiny heart.

Alice had rushed straight home from the café. She was dripping with sweat by the time she came through her studio door. She turned on the ceiling fan, which whirred and clanked and sent dust flying around the room, but the breeze it gave out was the only way she could bear to spend any length of time in her poky little studio. In the shower – this was in the days before Alice had become so fond of her long baths, but even if there had been a bath tub in that grotty little apartment, she would not have wanted to soak in it – Alice soaped every inch of her body, astonished at how her sensitive skin responded to her own touch. Her sudsy hand between her legs found a sensitive spot which made her cry out when she touched it. This new secret button was a revelation to her. She washed away all the juices that had dampened her panties over the last few hours, and was astonished to find that even as she towelled herself off she was producing more.

The images of things that she wanted to do to Jacques and the things that she wanted him to do to her were constantly playing in her head. It was as though she were trapped in a pornographic cinema where the film was played on a loop and she was the star as well as the audience member. In these constantly moving, flickering images, Alice saw herself face down on a bed, biting the pillow as Jacques' body, lean, sinewy and hard, moved on top of her. She saw her legs wrapped around his strong brown neck and his nose gently nuzzling her clit while his tongue fucked her pussy. When it came to sucking his dick, or having him penetrate her, the images became fuzzy and vague, as though pixelated by a censor. Alice had never been interested in the pornographic films and magazines that her schoolfriends had purloined from their boyfriends and brothers and watched in fits of screaming giggles. So she had no real idea what a hard-on looked like up close, and less idea what she would do with one. Would Jacques be able to tell that she had never had a lover before? If he guessed, would he care?

Alice pulled a pair of tiny lacy panties over her hips. They were sodden within seconds. She wore no bra, and slipped a simple turquoise sundress over her head, enjoying the feeling of the silk against her nipples. The bodice was fitted at the waist and the skirt flared out at the knee. When she had first bought it, Alice had fancied herself as the prim fifties starlet. But tonight she wore it with a different attitude, and even this innocent dress looked wanton and daring.

Alice turned off the ceiling fan and the light in her bedroom before making her way up the staircase that led to the front door. A shadeless light bulb swung on the ground-floor landing. Moths and mosquitoes danced a suicidal tango around its flickering glare. Alice took one last chance to catch her reflection in the age-spotted hallway mirror. Her fair hair was damply piled up on top of her head but already almost dry. She wore no make-up – she never did then – but her excitement had widened her pupils, giving her eyes a dark, dangerous glint, brought a blush to her cheeks and subtly swollen and darkened her lips.

As she tucked a stray tendril of hair behind her ear, she heard heavy footfalls coming down the stairs above her head. Her upstairs neighbours remained a complete mystery to her and if they were anything like as unpleasant as her immediate neighbour she didn't want to get to know them. As Alice fumbled with the bolt on the front door, the footsteps behind her came to a dead halt and there was a sharp intake of breath behind her. She froze. And then she heard her name spoken in a voice that was already as familiar to her as her own.

'Alice.' She turned around slowly, wondering how he had got into her building. Had he followed her? He asked her the same question. 'How did you know I lived here? How did you get in?' Then he saw her key, exactly the same as his, the same distinctive key fob and chunky bronze key which opened the master lock of the front door. They both realised at exactly the same time what had happened. Alice laughed with delight at the coincidence; Jacques did not crack a smile.

'Fate,' he said, nodding to himself. 'I should have known.' He descended the remaining few stairs. Alice noticed that while she had showered, he had not. The smell of his fresh sweat was sweeter to her than any cologne. Alice began to shiver uncontrollably and knew that they would never make it out to dinner.

Jacques placed one broad, masculine hand on Alice's right breast and cupped it. His hands dwarfed her small tits but even as he gently stroked the fabric of her dress, they began to come alive under his touch. Her nipples were so swollen now that they were almost as large as her breasts, bulging and puffy and pushing out the turquoise silk. With his thumb, he traced a circle around the swollen bud, watching Alice's face as she closed her eyes. Sliding his hand underneath her dress and sighing as the shoulder strap fell down to expose her right breast, Jacques suddenly clamped the nipple between his thumb and forefinger. Alice felt weak and strong at the same time.

'Come with me,' he said, and with Alice's nipple still gripped between his fingers, he turned around and walked up the stairs, leading her by the tender tip of her tit up three flights of stairs. He pulled the swollen nipple, stretching the tiny breast away from Alice's body, and his hand on her naked flesh felt like fire or ice, she couldn't tell which. The heat and wetness between her legs increased with every step up the rickety, dirty staircase. When he let go of her to let himself into his room, the pert flesh bounced back and he watched as her breast bobbed a couple of times like a buoy on the sea. Her rosy nipple had darkened to the colour of fuschia petals, and the swollen bud was marked with his fingerprints. Alice stood waiting, her whole body turned into a mass of hot liquid, unable to do anything until she felt his hands on her flesh again.

Jacques' room was high up enough to be able to escape the smells from the street and he had left the window wide open. A single sheer white curtain billowed in the evening breeze, but it was too dark to see anything else. The room smelt of his hair and skin and cigarettes. He took a lighter from his pocket and the single tiny flame soon gave life to a dozen candles, gently illuminating the darkness. Alice could make out a futon, carelessly draped with a petrol-blue chinoiserie bedspread. There were three mismatched chairs and a coffee table. Books. Piles and piles of paper. And lots of black wires and electronic equipment that meant nothing to Alice.

'I write,' said Jacques, as though those two words

summed up everything that happened in this room and everything he was. And again, he turned to Alice with that intense stare that paralysed her with fear and desire.

Alice's nerves returned. She had planned on spending a couple of hours talking to Jacques and eating and drinking with him before finding herself in this situation. She was suddenly aware that she was desperately hungry and would have given anything for a glass of wine. She felt that she was about to lose control of her body. Jacques seemed to sense this. He cupped her pale face in his hands. Alice felt her whole body turn to milk as he leaned in for their first kiss. His lips were soft and dry on hers, but his tongue was wet and probing, and he forced open her lips and deftly began to explore the cave of her mouth. Alice responded to his kisses with her own ravenous bites: as their mouths moved together in perfect understanding, she felt as though she were coming home. He talked as he kissed her, something Alice hadn't known was possible.

'It's been seven hours since I first saw you,' he said, her upper lip clenched between his teeth. 'I wanted to do this then. I wanted to throw you on the floor and fuck you, I didn't care who was watching, didn't you feel it, I know you did, I could smell your cunt, our bodies are supposed to be together.'

Alice had no words. She remained silent even as Jacques' hands gripped her hips and gently gathered up the silken folds of her dress until it was bunched around her waist. Alice broke away from him for a second, raised her hands over her head and tore off her dress, tugging her hair and ripping out an earring, but she didn't care. Jacques' hands were like a lion's paws as he clawed at her panties with fists and rolled them down her legs, stopping to press his face to the sodden cotton gusset and inhale deeply. When he came back up to kiss her, Alice could taste her own musk on his lips and nostrils. She was greedy for it and kissed him hard, lips, teeth and tongue clashing furiously. She wanted Jacques to be naked too, and tugged at his waistband. She was painfully aware that she was a virgin who had never had occasion to undo a man's belt before, and her fingers shook. She fumbled, unable to undo the buckle but desperate to free the straining erection that was pressed against her stomach through Jacques' jeans. But his hands took over and with lightning precision his belt was off and his trousers were around his ankles. Simultaneously Alice tore off his light linen shirt, a tiny plastic button flying across the room.

Alice's clit was ignited with desire as she took in the raw sexuality of his naked body. His tan only faded slightly around his arse and dick, and he had the kind of swimmer's body that is muscular and strong without being bulky. Alice's legs parted involuntarily and a shimmering slick of liquid ran down her inner thigh. Jacques traced it with his thumb, running the rough digit towards her pussy: his hand would be the first to touch her there.

Her throbbing clit eagerly anticipated his touch but instead he stood up again and used the tip of his penis to gently nuzzle at the swollen bud. Then he was inside her within seconds, his dick filling her up, threatening to split her in two. She screamed as a second of intense pain and a tearing sensation was replaced by the most intense pleasure she had ever known: his pubic bone pounded against her clit, while his prick pumped into her pussy. From nowhere, a rush of heat and motion consumed her, and Alice yielded to the convulsions of her first orgasm. Alice could see why the poets and playwrights called orgasm a little death: she lost complete control over her entire body as she came, and let her limbs go limp as the contractions washed over her. After that, she could only lean in Jacques' arms, helpless and floppy as a rag doll, supported only by his arms around her waist and the wall behind her. His climax was only seconds behind hers and his spunk shot into her, mingling with her own juices and a tiny trace of blood where he had claimed his virgin territory. Alice was beyond caring what Jacques thought, desperate only for her swollen cunt to recover so they could repeat the experience, but Jacques was deeply touched and wiped the tender flesh between Alice's legs clean with his discarded white shirt.

'I was your first,' he said, as though it were what he had been expecting all along. 'You're lucky. It's not always that beautiful. I told you, you were meant for me.'

They drifted into sleep on top of the shiny satin bedspread, wrapped in each other's arms. Alice woke at four in the morning to find that only two candles remained burning, but they cast enough light for her to see Jacques kneeling over her, a big hard-on outlined in silhouette.

'Open your mouth,' he said. She obeyed, and gratefully sucked his prick until she could taste his hot, salty spunk in her mouth. Instinct had taken over and she knew she needn't have worried about not knowing what to do with a naked man. When her body and Jacques' were together, a force greater than either of them took over and told her everything she needed to do. She lay on her back, licking the last of his spunk from her lips, sighed and parted her legs as he fell on all fours, teasing her clit to orgasm with a tongue that flickered over the swollen nub as quickly and lightly as a hummingbird's wing.

Alice remembered all this in vivid detail as she sat watching television with her husband in her sprawling Paris apartment. She recalled the nerves and the exhilaration of what had happened that night, how she had felt a kind of rebirth when their bodies came together, and echoes of that first flush of lust flooded her body now. But this time they

were tainted with a very real fear. Because Jacques knew
things about Alice that could destroy everything she had
worked for. She was frightened, out of her depth, uncom-
fortable. And, she had to admit to herself, she was also
wildly excited and felt more alive than she had done for
years.

CHAPTER FOUR

For the next two weeks, Alice and Jacques were fused together. At night, she would dream that he was inside her, screwing her so hard she could barely stand it, and she would wake to find that it was true. They barely ate, surviving on each other, wine and cigarettes. They rarely spoke, for what was the point of words when their bodies spoke each other's language so fluently? Attempts at conversations were made, but the sight of Jacques' mouth forming words was too much for Alice to resist. She would always have to lean in to kiss him, and to kiss him was to fuck him. They were parted only for the six hours a day that Alice spent at work and sometimes those six hours were punctuated by visits from Jacques which got riskier and riskier: first they fucked on a fire escape, then Alice crouched beneath Jacques' table and sucked his cock dry. She served customers across the counter with her legs spread and Jacques crouched between her knees, his fist firmly inside her pussy. Finally, during a brief moment when there were no customers but some might wander in at any moment, he bent her body over a table in a corner of the restaurant and fucked her from behind, squashing her tits against the surface of the table, forcing her to stand on her tiptoes to accommodate his thrusts and twisting his finger around in her arsehole as he penetrated her cunt so that she had to muffle her screams by biting down on her own forearm.

We use the phrase 'turned on' to describe intense desire, and that was how Alice felt: as though Jacques had flicked a switch somewhere inside her and sent electric currents flowing through her body. She felt that she had spent her whole life unplugged, half-alive. Now that Jacques was in her life and she was aware of all the amazing things her body and mind could do, she felt constantly turned on. Everything made her horny. The slow, deep beats and overtly sexual lyrics of hip-hop music blaring from a passing car would have Alice caressing her own collar-bone and pressing her legs together to squeeze her clitoris. Furniture was no longer just something to sit on, but something to recline on, squirm against, enjoying the feel of wood, velvet or metal against her skin. Now that she had come to know one body so intimately, other men were a source of fascination and wild attraction to her. Eye contact with even unattractive men, or the smell of customers' sweat or the rippling of a vein on a stranger's forearm would be enough to make her wonder what his prick looked like, and how it would feel inside her.

Even women turned her on. One day when Alice saw a voluptuous, coffee-skinned woman walking down the street in front of her with a tiny roll of fat visible between her tight T-shirt and her low-slung jeans, the sight of that squeezed-out flesh had been so compellingly erotic that she had slunk into an alleyway and masturbated furiously, making her two front fingers into a V-shape, placing a fingertip either side of her clit and rubbing hard, getting herself off in what seemed like the time it took to breathe in and breathe out. She had not even been able to wait for Jacques, who she knew would be lying on his bed, dick hard, waiting for her. Alice had been turned on, and sex was everywhere.

Gradually, they began to talk. Their bodies knew each other, but they were virtual strangers, and it was a strange process. She told him that she planned to be a great actress. He told her of film scripts he'd written, brilliant, daring stories which explored the limits of human experience and sexuality. They talked about books, plays and films, but talking would lead to touching, and touching to sex, and their conversations never lasted more than a couple of hours.

Jacques loved the fact that he was responsible for Alice's sexual awakening and she, in turn, was happy to be his plaything. The more dangerous his games became, the wilder and more alive she felt. She sat open-legged before a mirror while he used an old-fashioned cut-throat razor, bought specifically from an antique shop for the occasion, to shave her pussy bare, an experience she found so erotic that they were able to use her pussy juice instead of shaving cream to lubricate the blade's smooth path. He ordered her to steal a bottle of extra-virgin olive oil from work, and gently used it to loosen up her arsehole before sliding his cock into her back passage, simultaneously inserting the neck of the bottle into Alice's cunt, so that she felt that she would burst with pressure and pleasure. He taught her how to recline on the bed with her head hanging off and relax her gag reflex so that she could swallow the entire length of his dick, right up to his balls: he would fuck her face and massage her tits, holding up the nipples and then dropping them, watching her breasts jiggle while his length penetrated her throat, until she was as skilled as a circus sword-swallower. And always, after they had made each other come, he would say the same thing to her.

'I love you, Alice. I love fucking you and I love you. We are each other's destiny.'

But as the summer wore on, feelings of claustrophobia began to haunt Alice. She was worried that her physical dependence on Jacques was an addiction. She had shut out the world outside and, as her mother would have said, she had 'let herself go'. Her hair had not been cut, let alone blow-dried, for six weeks and was beginning to look torn and haggard. She wasn't eating well and was becoming scrawny. Her white skin was constantly covered in scratches and bite marks, and because sex had replaced sleep, dark circles formed under her eyes. Her bush, usually so carefully waxed and shaped, grew unruly and wild: Jacques liked it that way, telling her that the hairier she was, the more he could smell the sweetness of her pussy.

And soon, real life began to creep back in. Alice had no telephone at her studio, but she could not ignore the daily letters from her parents begging her to contact them and make arrangements about starting her course in Paris. Alice's ambitious streak began to rear its head again. The life she was living here with Jacques was intense, claustrophobic and deeply enlivening. She could not have hoped for a better introduction to the ways of making love, and perhaps she would never find a lover like Jacques again. But it was incompatible with the discipline and hard work she needed to put in to make it as an actress. She had had enough of being a waitress; she was sick of waiting to be discovered, she was eager to get to drama school. Jacques was an artist, too. She was sure he would understand.

When she tried explaining this to Jacques, he didn't understand. He despised formal education, and when she told him that drama school was the only route to an agent, he sneered at her for 'playing the game'. This conflict was the source of their first bitter argument. They had just finished making love up against the window of Jacques' room, Alice's body wrapped in the white curtain and pressed against the glass, Jacques' dick entering her from behind, and they had willed passers-by to look up and witness them. After they had both come, Jacques wrapped Alice so tightly in the cotton curtain that she felt trapped, like a mummy. She fought her way out of the bonds and screamed at him.

'I'm losing myself in you, Jacques!' cried Alice. Like her desire, her anger bubbled to the surface and spilled out. 'We never see anybody but each other. My life is working as a waitress, and fucking you. It's like drowning in honey. It's too much, we can't live like this for ever, we have no friends, we should be seeing other people, we can't just live on our dreams like this.'

Jacques gave her a wounded look as though she had kicked him in the balls. 'You want us to be like every other urban couple, having cosy dinner parties and talking about house prices? Fuck you and fuck that. You and I, Alice, are destined for a life less ordinary.'

'That's not what I said. That's not what I meant. It just gets a bit claustrophobic, only ever being with each other.'

'Well, you are all I'll ever want,' Jacques barked. 'But if I'm not enough for you, I'll find you some fucking friends.' His footsteps thudded angrily down the flight of stairs and the door's violent slam left the whole building shaking.

Alice was left naked on the bed feeling angry and confused. These feelings threatened to overwhelm her; she was in too deep. She returned to her own bedroom and tried to sleep, but she was wild with anger and frustration as well. Her body was already craving another fix of Jacques' cock, and like an addict, she couldn't relax until she had her hit.

At three o'clock in the morning, the door slammed shut for the second time. Jacques' voice, accompanied by two others that Alice didn't recognise, drifted down the staircase into Alice's room and woke her up. She leapt out of bed, threw on some clothes and took the stairs two at a time, to find Jacques standing on the landing with two strangers he introduced as Francis and Julie.

The couple she saw standing at the top were so good-looking they took Alice's breath away. Francis was mixed race, a good head taller than Jacques, with cocoa-brown skin and a physique that looked as though it had been carved in mahogany. He wore a T-shirt with the Brazilian flag on it, denim cut-offs, beads around his neck and wrists and his hair was tightly knotted into short dreadlocks. The woman who stood next to him was the sexiest female Alice had ever seen. Julie had the alabaster skin of the natural redhead, smattered with freckles on her nose and shoulders. She was tall for a woman, only slightly shorter than Jacques, and was the dictionary definition of an hourglass figure. Dainty ankles swelled into shapely legs, which led to a generous arse and thighs, barely covered by a mini sarong that looked like it might have been a sari in its previous life. Her tiny waist was the same size as Alice's but thrown into stark contrast by a pair of round, full, pendulous breasts which were struggling to be contained by the red bikini top she wore. Like Francis, Julie wore a lot of jewellery, but while his wooden beads were the same colour as his brown skin, her wrists, ears, ankles and neck were draped with chains and baubles in clashing metallic colours; silvers, golds, coppers and bronzes cast tiny brilliant lights on to Julie's fair skin. Her facial features were strong, fleshy and sensual. A wise, full mouth was a natural dark red without the aid of make-up and huge, round greeny-grey eyes lit up her face. Compared with Julie, Alice felt faded and washed out. The length and texture of Julie's vivid red hair Alice could not see as it was coiled tightly on top of her head, held in place with a chopstick. Alice wanted to see that hair unleashed more than anything, and had to fight her desire to pull out of the chopstick, run her fingers through Julie's hair and let it fall over her shoulders. She made do with a chaste, social kiss on the cheek.

Alice was torn between happiness at new people to socialise with – like normal couples did – and disappointment that this unexpected company meant she wouldn't get to fuck Jacques again tonight. The four retired to Jacques' bedroom for the ritual of lighting the candles and opening the wine. There was nowhere for all of them to sit but on the bed. Francis and Julie were playful and flirtatious, and made a refreshing change from Jacques' brooding intensity. It turned out that they were not established friends of Jacques' but a couple he had picked up in a bar. Julie was a source of fascination. Her lips were stained a dark berry colour by the red wine, and Alice found that she wanted to lick it off. To kiss Julie, place her tongue between those damson lips and probe all the corners of her mouth. She was surprised at the strength of the attraction, and wondered if Jacques could read the familiar signs of her arousal – glittering eyes, flushed cheeks and erect nipples, which Alice tried to cover by folding her arms over her chest.

But when Alice saw Francis and Jacques look to the women, then back at each other, and raise their eyebrows, she suddenly understood that she was not the only one feeling a sexual charge. Before she could think about how to make a move on Julie, Jacques leaned across the bed and kissed Alice as though they were the only two people in the room. Alice was aware of Francis and Julie's eyes on them as her nipples poked out from beneath her dress and Jacques guided her hand to his fly so that she could feel his burgeoning hard-on.

Soft sucking sounds and gentle movement from the other side of the bed told her that Francis and Julie were also kissing. While Jacques' teeth clamped down on to the skin of her shoulder and he began to give her a love bite, she feasted her eyes on the other couple, brown skin on white flesh as they began to move and rise. Barely knowing what she was doing, Alice reached a hand across the bed and her fingers found Julie's arm. She began to trail her nails up and down the soft skin on the inside of Julie's elbow. Julie's sighs grew louder. As if by prior agreement, Jacques and Francis disentangled themselves from their women and sat back on the bed, watching the proceedings unfold. Alice knelt opposite Julie and crawled towards her, while Julie did the same. Alice and Julie crouched opposite each other, tentatively squeezing one another's tits, Alice delighting in the way Julie's bulbous breasts squeezed out between her fingers, Julie revelling in Alice's firm, pointed tits. Their knees bashed together and their pussies were touching, smooth lips brushing against silky clits, their liquids mingling.

Alice was dimly aware of Jacques running to the edge of the room and trailing a camera on her. She played up to it, pulling Julie's hair so that she fell on to her back and riding her body like a surfer on a board, grinding her clit into the other woman's soft mound of Venus and spreading her legs so that the camera could see her pink, glistening hole, a hole that was aching for a man even while she wrapped herself around a woman. She could sense Francis and Jacques moving in the background but could only focus on Julie's body and the camera, the permitted voyeur which made an already intense experience almost unbearably charged.

The sight of Julie and Alice pleasuring each other was too strong a pull for the men and soon all four bodies came together again. Alice closed her eyes and let the sensations wash over her as Francis's hard body pressed against Julie's soft one, and when she felt hands gripping her clit and pulling apart her pussy she kept her eyes closed tightly. The thrilling part was not knowing who was touching her. But there was no mistaking Jacques' dick, nudging at her lips one minute and then, when she opened her mouth to receive it, teasingly withdrawing and slapping her cheek as her mouth gasped for his length. Then a sudden movement and he was on her, inside her, fucking her while Francis and Julie's hands caressed her neck, arms, feet, legs. All four of them crawled over each other, hungry mouths biting and licking whatever they could get, drifting in and out of sleep and orgasm.

Alice did not remember falling asleep, but she woke

with a dry mouth and thumping headache. Her body was sore all over, spent by the force of two intense climaxes. She felt the way she used to at school when she had swum a kilometre, or done a long cross-country run. She surveyed the scene. Francis and Julie lay side by side but not touching on the half-bare mattress, their perfect young bodies looking like a pair of brackets facing one another. Jacques remained asleep, exhaustion and deep sleep softening the features which had been twisted into expressions of rapture just a couple of hours ago. He had one arm slung over the pillow. Alice could still see the imprint that her head and body had made on the bedclothes. All of a sudden, what she had done shocked her. She had a sudden clarity of vision, and knew that this must not be allowed to happen again. She wanted more than anything to get out of the room, because she knew that if she stayed, she would wake up and never do anything the rest of her life but remain here and enjoy those sensations again and again and again. It would be so easy to forego the life that she had planned for herself and stay here. But Alice knew that even she and Jacques would not be able to survive on dreams, sex and a waitress's meagre wages. Better to end the whole thing now and preserve the summer as a perfect memory.

Self-preservation was the overriding instinct as she picked up her clothes from the four corners of the room and slowly, carefully, silently put them back on. Alice turned her attention towards the video camera. She pressed the eject button. The tape slid noiselessly out of the machine, and Alice held it in her hand, aware of the magnitude of what she was about to do. Bending down, she kissed the sleeping Jacques goodbye for ever, closed the door behind her with the softest of clicks, and ran barefoot down the stairs to her basement room, one finger unhooking the shiny black tape from its reel and pulling at first an inch and then a yard and then what seemed like miles and miles and miles of black ribbon, the magnetic strip that contained the images of four bodies fucking. Alice closed her fist around the tape and crunched it, tore it with her hands as she ran, made it into a ball and wrapped it round and round the now empty cassette. She threw her clothes and the few books she had brought with her into the battered holdall she had arrived with. Without thinking about the lost deposit on her rented room, or the job she was due to give up in a week anyway, she left the building for ever.

The first train of the day to Paris was leaving in forty minutes. Feeling giddy and mad, Alice bought herself a first-class ticket with the credit card her parents had given her for emergencies and made her way to the platform. Even at this early hour, heatwaves shimmered in the distance and distorted the view. The sun beat down on her bare skin, reviving the smells of last night's adventures. She bought a bottle of mineral water and locked herself into the tiny station washroom where she gave herself an impromptu shower, pouring two litres of volcanically filtered water over her head and running the tiny bar of soap between her legs and under her arms.

Her cleansed body was a metaphor for the life she intended to live from now on: fresh, focused, in control. A tiny voice in her head was screaming at her to turn back before it was too late. She let ambition and excitement about her career drown it out.

Alice's first-class seat faced in the direction of travel as the train pulled out of the station. Forward, not back, thought Alice. From now on, I only look forward.

CHAPTER FIVE

Alice decided to treat herself to a glass of champagne and a plate of oysters to celebrate her escape and, delving into her bag, found a drama textbook she had been meaning to study all summer but had not opened. She had an amazing experience under her belt; now it was simply a question of learning the discipline of acting. As she sipped the cool, dry, crisp champagne, Alice silently toasted her future career. It would be hard-going without sex for a few months but men needed to slide down her list of priorities for a while. It was time to concentrate on herself.

At the end of the meal she was surprised to find her bill had been settled. She looked around the carriage, wondering who could have been so generous. She hoped that it was the distinguished-looking gentleman in the crisp suit and the open-necked shirt, nursing a glass of red wine and sneaking glances at Alice over the top of his copy of *Le Figaro*. His sandy hair, broad muscular build and light tan could not have been more different from Jacques' wiry, intense sexuality, and there was something solid and appealing about his good looks. And he was immaculately dressed and groomed; his French polish made a refreshing change to Jacques' scruffy bohemian air. Alice raised one quizzical eyebrow in his direction.

'Do I have you to thank for my meal?' she asked him.

'I hope you'll forgive me,' he said, and his voice was smooth and fruity, like the wine he drank. 'I saw a beautiful woman reading a book about the theatre, and I always like to help the struggling actress in any way I can.'

'I'm not even struggling yet,' said Alice. 'I start drama school in a couple of weeks.'

'Your voice is very charming,' he said wistfully. 'I could listen to you for hours. Why don't you join me at my table?'

Alice was pleased to slide into the plush red seat and examine her new friend across the polished walnut table. Up close, Alice could see that he was slightly older than she had first thought — in his mid- to late-thirties – and she welcomed his confidence and his dry sense of humour. As the French countryside rolled by, the man asked her with great interest about her prospective career, the course she was taking, and the kind of work she wanted to do as an actress. Alice almost felt as though she were being interviewed for a job. He kept the conversation professional but Alice couldn't help wondering what the pinstriped material of his trousers concealed. She thought she saw a promising bulge nestled against the top of his right thigh. She thought of Jacques' dick, and the idea of living without it caused an anguished pang between her legs. She felt her nipples stiffen and folded her arms, trying to disguise her arousal, but she only succeeded in pushing her breasts closer together and emphasising her cleavage. The man opposite her was too much of a gentleman to leer, but she noticed him shifting uncomfortably in his seat.

As the train pulled into Paris, Alice explained that she would be going home to her parents now to collect her things but that she would be back in Paris to move into her new flat in about ten days.

'Have you any friends in the city?' said her new companion. Alice shook her head. 'Well, then,' he went on, effortlessly hauling a heavy leather suitcase down from the overhead rack, his shirt sleeve tightening over a bulging bicep, 'I would very much like to take you to dinner and get to know you a little better.' Then he gave a surprised laugh. 'This is ridiculous; we don't even know each other's names.'

'It's Alice. Alice Hill.'

'Alice Hill,' he said, fishing in his suit trouser pocket for a card and a Mont Blanc fountain pen. He offered the card to her, blank side up, and Alice wrote her full name and her mother's telephone number on the back of it. 'If something terrible happens to me and I lose your number, here is another card so you know where to find me.' He handed it to Alice. When she read the name, she let out an involuntary gasp. For she had spent the last six hours in conversation with Pierre Daumier, arthouse film director and winner of the Palm D'Or at the previous year's Cannes Film Festival. Alice had seen every one of his films and admired him hugely.

'I'm so sorry, I didn't recognise you,' said Alice. 'I feel rather foolish.'

'There's no reason why you would,' said Pierre. 'Not if I'm doing my job properly. After all, my place is behind the camera. It's beautiful girls like you who should be in front of it.' Alice liked the way his smile showed up the fine lines around his eyes. His friendliness and authority was refreshing after Jacques' tortured-artist act.

Alice and Pierre said goodbye on the station concourse with a single kiss on either cheek. When his lips touched her skin, there was none of the sizzling electricity that had characterised the first flesh-on-flesh contact with Jacques. But perhaps that's a good thing, thought Alice. After all, I couldn't have gone through life a slave to my passions. It could be a good thing for me.

Over the next year, Pierre Daumier proved to be a very good thing indeed for Alice Hill. True to his word, he called her in London two days after their meeting on the train and arranged to take her out to dinner at La Coupole on her first night in Paris.

'I noticed that you like champagne and oysters, and this place does the best in town,' he said. Their courtship could not have been more different to the whirlwind of lust and danger that she had known with Jacques. For a whole year – the time it took Alice to complete her drama course – she had dinner with Pierre once a week, and he never once tried to kiss her. But there developed an unspoken understanding that she was his. Not only that they would become a couple, but that they would work together as soon as Alice's studies were completed.

'I've been looking for a muse all my life, Alice,' said Pierre over cocktails at a restaurant one evening. 'And I think you will be that muse. But there is no hurry. You must study first. The skills and experiences you will learn this year will shape the acting you do for the rest of your life. There are many young actresses who drop out of drama school for a part. Their careers are always the poorer for it. No, Alice, I want to nurture this wonderful talent of yours.'

Alice did not tell her fellow students that she was friends with Pierre Daumier. When his name appeared in the trade press or his latest project was reviewed, she had to use all her willpower to stop screaming excitedly, 'I know him!' So her fellow students knew nothing of Pierre

– and he knew nothing of her relationships with her fellow students. Alice took a string of lovers, desperate to satisfy the need in her that Jacques had awoken, and although none of the men she slept with – fellow students mainly, the odd guy picked up in a nightclub – came close to making her feel the way Jacques had, she found that closing her eyes and picturing her former lover could often tip her over the edge into orgasm. But Pierre could not disapprove, because Pierre did not know. And her friends could not be jealous of Pierre because they did not know about him. It was the perfect arrangement.

Alice completed her course in June, and Pierre offered to take her on holiday to celebrate the end of her studies and the beginning of her life as a working actress. He suggested the south of France, but Alice shook her head violently and said that she would prefer to go somewhere altogether different. They went to Italy, where they spent a week in adjoining rooms of a suite in a sumptuous Florence hotel. They ate at the finest restaurants every night and finally discussed specific future film projects: Pierre had a lead role for Alice in a series of literary adaptations he had recently bought the rights to. Alice thrilled at the thought.

Pierre impressed her with his knowledge of art. At the Uffizi Gallery, he was as informative as any tour guide. He stood Alice in front of 'The Birth Of Venus', that great Botticelli painting showing a porcelain-skinned maiden with long flowing hair the colour of wheat emerging naked from a huge seashell.

'I think this painting is the most erotic image I've ever seen,' said Pierre. 'She reminds me of you.' In over a year of friendship, this was the closest he had ever come to making a pass at her. That night, when they were walking over the Pontevecchio, Alice looked up at him and willed him to kiss her. He lowered his mouth to hers and pressed it, shaking with tension and emotion. It was an exquisite kiss, tender, respectful, gentle, and Alice felt aroused in a very different way to how she had done with Jacques. This was butterflies-in-the-tummy lust, a comforting, gentle desire that would delight but not overwhelm her.

They made love the first time that night. Pierre led her by the hand to his hotel room and undressed her slowly, taking time between the removal of each garment to kiss her on her lips, her neck, her knees, her inner thighs. Arousal washed over her and receded again in gentle waves. When she was naked apart from bra and panties, he picked her up and carried her to his huge bed where he slid the straps down over her shoulders and scooped her breasts out of the cups of her bra, tenderly unfastening the back clasp, and hanging her bra neatly over the back of the chair before returning to her body. Crouching on all fours, he bent down and kissed each nipple with tenderness and reverence. This slow, methodical, almost worshipful method of foreplay was a revelation to Alice. As Pierre's tongue gently licked the underside of her breasts, she could feel a butterfly flutter stirring her clitoris and when she felt him rolling her panties down over her hips, his warm breath on her inner thigh and then over her ever moistening pussy, she felt the tension build and knew that a delicious eruption was on its way. The featherlight strokes of Pierre's tongue on her clitoris teased her almost to orgasm but she wanted to come with him inside her and pushed his head away.

'What's the matter, darling?' asked Pierre, his face a mask of concern

'Nothing. Everything you're doing is perfect. But I want you inside me. Come here.'

And Alice pulled the crouching man up towards her, kissing him deep and hard and tasting her own pussy juices as she did so. For a moment she was reminded of the sweet honey of Julie's cunt on her lips and let out an involuntary moan of pleasure. Close up, she could admire Pierre's body. Unthinkable that they had known each other so well for a year and yet this was the first time she had seen just how broad and well developed his arms were, the bulky tone of his pecs framing a smooth, biscuit-coloured chest with a six-pack of rippled muscle that had been hiding underneath his designer suits all this time. Next to him she felt feminine, vulnerable, protected. He drew out an entirely different kind of sexuality to the wildcat wantonness that Jacques had unleashed in her.

Pierre's hard, thick cock was as stocky and satisfying as the rest of his body. Gently, he prodded the opening to her pussy then parted the lips, inserted the tip of his dick inside her, held it there for a few tantalising seconds and then thrust himself deep into her, stretched her inside. Alice enjoyed the sweet surrender. Ever the gentleman, Pierre concentrated on her own pleasure rather than his, and thrust his cock in and out of her slowly, building her climax up with a steady succession of thrusts. His trick of withdrawing his penis almost all the way out before putting his weight behind it and spearing her again was deliciously teasing. Pierre propped himself up on his right elbow and slid his left hand between his pubic bone and her pussy. Parting her damp blonde bush, he found her clitoris and gently stroked it, this double stimulation of pussy and cunt finally awakening the hot torrents of lust that Alice had missed for the last year. She let out a low moan and let rip.

'Fuck me. Oh, fuck me. I need your cock in me. Your big dick, deeper! Deeper! Fuck me. I need it so bad. Deeper, harder.' And she bucked her hips, digging her nails into his arse, grinding her clit into his pubic hair and feeling the delicious friction, pushing her hips so hard against his and knowing there would be bruises the next day but not caring about that right now. All she cared about was getting his cock as deep inside her as they could manage.

She sang and swore as the orgasm took her over and felt her pussy muscles massaging and hugging Pierre's dick, so that his climax was hot on the heels of hers.

'That's it, baby,' cajoled Alice. 'Fill me with spunk. Pump it in. Oh, my pussy needs it.' He closed his eyes, a vein on his forehead bulged then receded, and Alice watched as his face was ironed out by the release of tension. No woman ever truly knows a man until she has seen his orgasm face, she thought.

'Oh, Pierre,' sighed Alice, as her pussy continued to convulse around his still-twitching hard-on. 'I've waited for that for a year.' She met his eyes and was shocked by the expression in them – a mixture of shock, disappointment and revulsion. 'What's the matter? Didn't you like it?'

Pierre's reply was murmured into her shoulder. 'Oh, Alice. Darling Alice. It was the most exquisite sex I've ever had. It's just that you have rather taken me aback with your, um, your language. I've never been spoken to quite like that by a lady before.' His disapproval was implicit in the tone of his voice. Alice was slightly shocked, because Jacques had loved it when she was loud and explicit and yelled all the things she wanted to do and everything she was feeling in pornographic detail. And her other lovers – those who had managed to elicit such a response in her – had always been really turned on by her dirty talk, telling her that it was madly horny to see such a polished, elegant woman swearing like a sailor. But her experience had also taught her that one man's aphrodisiac is another man's turn-off. Alice sighed and inwardly resolved to stay silent and compliant during future lovemaking sessions with Pierre.

She stroked his face, feeling that an explanation or apology was in order. 'It's only that I wanted you so very, very much. You should take it as a compliment. But if you're not comfortable with it, I won't shout like that again.'

Pierre nodded drowsily; he was struggling to stay awake, a pattern that Alice would soon realise repeated itself every time he made love. He did not reply to her and was soon fast asleep, his retreating dick pooling in his own spunk inside her pussy. Alice wriggled out from under him and gazed down at her sleeping Adonis, running her fingers through the fuzz of hair on his chest. After sex, the last thing she wanted to do was go to sleep. She never felt more alive, never felt more like seizing all the world had to offer, never felt more like talking.

She had not been lying when she said it was the best

sex she had had in a year: it was far and away the best fuck she'd had since that last one with Jacques. She had definitely enjoyed Pierre's body and his respectful, diligent style of foreplay was unlike anything else she had ever known. And so what if his reaction to her outburst was a little concerning? She would learn to bite her lip.

She covered Pierre with the golden brocade eiderdown of the hotel bed and lay beside him, feeling a sense of security that gave her surprising comfort. Despite the energy that was buzzing about her body, she drifted off to sleep with her head on his chest. To her astonishment, when she woke it was seven o'clock in the morning and Pierre too was stirring. They kissed sleepily.

'Am I awake, or was last night a dream?' Pierre mumbled. His morning erection was thick and growing by the second. Alice put out her hand to cup his balls, and slid her fingers slowly up the shaft of his cock.

'I would say you're very much awake,' she replied, and before he had a chance to respond, she gently pushed back his hips so that he was lying on his back. She slung one leg over his prone body and lowered her cunt, already wet with anticipation, on to his engorged flesh, watching his face go from sleepy softness to hard, urgent lust in the time it took for the inside of her pussy to wrap itself around the dick and squeeze it hard. Last night's long, drawn-out sex had been delicious, but the animal in Alice was now in the mood for something hard and thrillingly fast. She bounced up and down, enjoying the feel of Pierre's prick expanding inside her pussy. The sight of her bouncing tits, topped by puffy pink nipples, transfixed him. Hooking her arm under his thigh, she raised it up, pulling him deeper inside her, and guided his hand on to her clitoris, which was already slippery from her own juices. Pierre circled his fingers around the flesh of the sensitive little bud, making her laugh with pleasure, before giving it a playful little flick that triggered her orgasm. She rode the climax out, moving her upper body backwards and forwards as a delicious tingling spread throughout her clit, cunt, tits, arms, legs, fingers, toes and lips. Careful to keep her moans of pleasure wordless, she leaned forward, extending her legs behind her, and lowering her upper body until her head was level with his. Her blonde hair tickled his chest and shoulders, and she kissed him while he came, his hot breath filling her mouth and his spunk filling her pussy. Now it was her turn to collapse on top of him, enjoying the light layer of sweat that lay between her tits and his chest. She looked into his eyes, safe in the knowledge that if he wasn't hers before, he certainly was now.

'I love you, Alice,' breathed Pierre, his voice breaking. 'I'm so in love with you. I want to spend the rest of my life with you – you're my muse and I want you to be my lover for the rest of my life. Will you marry me?' Alice answered him with a sweet, slow kiss. This time Pierre didn't fall asleep.

Eight years later, Alice was still Pierre's muse, but the film projects had become safer and more commercial: Pierre was seduced by the Hollywood dollar, and the daring, art-house projects they had discussed when they had first met had turned into bland romantic comedies that were hits internationally, not just in France. Alice could never work out which came first, her disillusionment with Pierre the director or her disillusionment with Pierre her husband, but she did know that neither her career nor her marriage had made her feel alive for years.

CHAPTER SIX

It was a week before the next letter came. During those seven days, Alice often had the feeling that she was being followed. She turned around to look behind her so many times that her neck began to ache. But she never saw Jacques.

She had final proof that he was indeed following her when the next letter arrived, this time not pushed under her front door, but slipped in her bag. Her fingers closed over the smooth paper as she was fumbling for her front door key and she knew without looking what this foreign object in her handbag was. She tried to think of all the places she had been that day. When had he done it? When she was browsing at the cosmetics counter in Les Galeries Lafayette? When she was hailing a taxi? When she was smoking a cigarette and people-watching in a café in Montmartre?

There had been a time when her body would have recognised Jacques' presence from a distance of ten, maybe twenty, metres. She would have been shivering and shaking but that had not happened today. Or had it? Since that first blue letter announcing that Jacques was back in her life she had been switched back on again, so that every tiny, everyday experience was suffused with sexuality and erotic potential. She had even found herself unable to keep her hands off her husband, something Pierre had not minded the first two successive nights she had taken his cock between her lips because her hands couldn't get him hard enough quick enough. However, on the third day he had pushed her away. The rejection had stung Alice, not because Pierre had turned her down but because she needed a cock in her so badly it was almost a pain. It had almost killed her to wait until Pierre was asleep before opening her bedroom door and rocking herself to orgasm with the solid silver dildo she kept wrapped in a silk scarf in her lingerie drawer for the occasions when fingers were not enough and she needed to feel something inside her.

Still fingering the paper square in her handbag, Alice walked through the empty lobby and began to ascend the marble staircase that wrapped around the lift shaft and ran through the centre of the building. The ancient iron cage was descending with its usual din. As the lift passed her, Alice waved hello to a pair of neighbours visible through the grille.

When they were out of sight, she pulled the envelope from her bag and held it to her nose, wondering if it bore a trace of his scent. It carried no odour, and with a pang Alice realised that she could not remember Jacques' smell. A neighbour on the staircase was almost keeping pace with her. Only when he raised his eyebrows and winked at her did she realise that she had been inadvertently fondling her own breast and that her nipples were hard.

Outside her front door, Alice opened the envelope, not wanting Pierre to see it and question her. The note was briefer this time.

Meet me at Café St Giles, 7th Arrondisement at 3 p.m. tomorrow

No 'Dear Alice', no please, no signature. Jacques was obviously completely confident that Alice would obey his summons. He was right to be.

The next day, Alice showered and scented herself and made herself up as though attending a premiere rather than having coffee with an old boyfriend in a café in an unglamorous part of town. She was frightened by the menacing tone of Jacques' letter but could not deny that whenever she thought of him a pulse began to beat between her legs. Unable to stay in the apartment because she was so restless, she hailed a taxi to a chic district and had her hair professionally blow-dried. The hairdresser chatted to her about fashion and frocks and her husband, mentioning a recent interview they had done together. Alice wondered if it was significant that she should be reminded of her public life with Pierre in the moments before going to see Jacques.

The tabac that Jacques had chosen overlooked a pretty, leafy square but had a shabby sleaziness about it that was in keeping with his personality. She looked at her white-gold watch. She was five minutes early. Good. She got to choose where they sat, and could select a discreet table where they would not be bothered by autograph hunters or, worse, journalists. She was in luck. A red, leather-lined booth in the corner of the tabac was positioned so that while it was easy to see into the room, most of the other customers had their backs to the table. She beckoned the waiter over and ordered an espresso. Then, realising that this was a mistake – her pulse was already racing a mile a minute – she instead chose a hot chocolate. When her drink arrived, she wrapped her hands around the tall glass cup for comfort as well as warmth and to steady her hands.

The door creaked open, a few leaves blew in and there he was. Alice felt something between desire and nausea. The furrow between his eyes was deeper, and his hair was shorter around the sides. He had gained a little weight, but it suited him: his jawline was softer and he was no longer too thin for his height. As he walked towards her, intense but half-smiling, that dark lock of hair fell into his eyes again and Alice could see that it was shot through with a couple of strands of gun-metal grey. And, God, he was as beautiful, if not more beautiful than she remembered him.

Before they had a chance to speak, she noticed something else. The shabbiness of his jeans, the threadbare shirt and the worn leather of his jacket told her that he was still poor, poor as when they met. Unlike her, he had not found his fortune. She was the international success, but he remained a struggling artist. Her stomach lurched, from disappointment not desire, as she realised that he was probably there to get some money out of her. After all, he had every reason to be angry with her. She had left him without a word of explanation, although she was sure he had guessed the reason. But asking for money? Was that really the best way to get his revenge? Unsure whether he was about to attack or charm her, she steeled herself and tried to ignore the fact that her breath was coming in short sharp gasps and that her panties were becoming damp.

'Alice.' He breathed the word. She held out her cheeks for a formal kiss hello and when his lips touched her cheek, she felt a slight wetness of his mouth, and did he scrape that stubble along her cheek deliberately? He knew that the most sensitive part of her body was the skin around her mouth – he would not have been able to resist.

'Hello, Jacques.'

He broke into a smile, that same smile which had been such a rare treat when they were together. The teeth were still so white, the tongue still so pink and the lips had lost none of their fleshy, sensuous attractiveness in the last eight years. Alice had a sudden, vivid image of where that mouth had been, remembered the eyes that were meeting her own now gazing up at her from between her legs while his nose nuzzled her clitoris, his tongue probed her cunt, and his thumb slid in and out of her arsehole. She did not realise her mouth had fallen open until Jacques leaned over and used his thumb and forefinger to close her parted lips. She saw that he had a drop of chocolate, presumably from her lips, on his finger. Slowly, deliberately, he slid his finger in and out of his mouth.

'Stop it, Jacques,' admonished Alice. 'You can't behave like that around me. It's not appropriate. I'm married.'

'Oh, I know that you're married. I've been following your progress. You've done very well for yourself since you were begging to suck my cock in an attic flat, haven't you, darling?' The bitterness in his voice broke her heart. Jacques looked over his shoulder and mouthed an order to the waiter. An awkward few seconds passed. 'Of course, I was co-starring the first time you were ever committed to film, wasn't I?'

She thought back to that last night when she had fled Cannes with nothing but a tiny suitcase and a shredded black videotape. The film that she had destroyed before anyone had a chance to view it.

'I'm sorry, but you do understand why I had to do it, don't you? I had to think of myself, and my future. I hoped you would understand and think of me the way I think of you, fondly. I was drowning in you, Jacques. Your games were getting darker, you were like an addiction, and the only way to really break an addiction is to go cold turkey, so that's what I did.' She was babbling now, but she couldn't stop. 'And I had to take the film. I don't regret what we did; I had a great night. I had a great summer, but I was ambitious, Jacques. I couldn't have a tape around that could surface in years to come and ruin my career.'

Jacques stared into his coffee. 'You could have trusted me.'

'No, I couldn't.'

Jacques opened his mouth.

He seemed as if he was about to say something but then thought better of it and changed tack.

'What's it like?' he asked. Alice knew exactly what he was referring to, but feigned innocence.

'What's what like?' she said.

'With Pierre,' he said simply. 'Sex with Pierre. I can imagine you, my lithe little Alice, suffocating under his weight, tolerating his cock, making all the right noises and then thinking of me when you come.'

This was so devastatingly near to the truth that Alice felt tears prick her eyes but she regained her composure in time to retort, 'I'm not your little Alice.'

'Have you ever felt as alive as you did that last night? I bet you haven't lost control of yourself since then, have you, Alice?'

She was close to losing control now. Despite all her efforts at steeling herself against Jacques' presence, she was beginning to melt, her body beginning to thrum and pulse and her pussy to swell and dampen. She felt Jacques' knee between hers. She withdrew her legs and clamped her knees shut.

'I'm going to go now, Jacques,' said Alice. But she stayed where she was, ignoring the voice in her head that told her to get up and walk away now. Alice Daumier the actress did not behave like this. She was calm and cool and did not let men like Jacques play games with her and feel her up in grubby little cafés. From her bag she fished out a ten euro note, placed it on the table and made to leave.

'You're not going anywhere,' said Jacques.

'I can't do this, Jacques,' Alice replied, standing up and wrapping her trenchcoat around her like armour. 'You can't make me.'

Alice turned on her heel and prepared to leave the café. Jacques' next words were spoken in such a low voice as to be barely audible but their meaning froze her in her tracks. 'I've still got a copy of the film.'

Alice spun around as though an invisible pair of hands had been placed on her shoulders and turned her body 180 degrees. Hadn't she destroyed the tape with her own hands?

'You're bluffing,' she managed to say, although she knew that bluffing wasn't Jacques' style. Jacques never said anything unless he meant it.

'Darling Alice,' he said, the smile on his pink lips genuine now that he could see he had her attention and indeed the upper hand in his little game. 'You really were very naive back then, weren't you? I might have only been starting out as a filmmaker, but I knew the basics. You never shoot a film using just one camera, you have at least two different cameras so you can capture the action from every angle. Sure, the tape you took would have had the best shot of your beautiful body and it was up close with you and Julie. But I had a secondary camera in place on the other side of the room. I have half an hour of footage that will show the entire world exactly the kind of person Alice Daumier really is.'

'I don't believe you,' she said.

Jacques opened his jacket and from the inside pocket produced a loose sheaf of photographic papers. With a quick glance around the café to make sure they were out of anyone's eyesight, he spread them on the table before her. Alice's stomach churned as she took in the grainy pictures, obviously stills taken from a film. The images of the four bodies entwined brought back the memories of that night more vividly than ever and despite her fear and stress, she found herself becoming incredibly aroused. With shaking hands, she picked up the photograph of herself and Julie, Alice, the slim blonde teenager, kneeling before Julie's statuesque beauty. Julie's beautiful head was thrown back, her bee-stung lips parted in ecstasy and her long red hair curled down her back like a nest of snakes. How well Alice could remember the feel and taste of Julie's bulbous breast in her mouth, the way she got greedier and greedier and couldn't get enough of it. How fascinated Alice had been by the contrast between the soft, plentiful flesh of the breast and the tiny but rock-hard nipples. She could smell Julie's perfume and recall the smattering of freckles across her breasts.

Alice placed the photo face down on the counter, unable to look at it any more, but Jacques had other ideas. The next photo he showed her was of the two of them, doing what they did best. He was sucking her as she lay back on the bed with her head thrown over the side of it, hair hanging down, his arms pinning her arms to the bed. At once she remembered how helpless she had felt with her body trapped under his like that, and realised that nothing before or since had ever compared to the moments when she had utterly surrendered herself to the overwhelming force of Jacques' desire. She was getting wetter by the second: her panties were saturated, and her inner thighs became damp and sticky. Alice shifted uncomfortably, allowing her knees to part again as she did so. Quick as a flash, Jacques placed his knee between her thighs and forced them open. She could feel her clit swell and rise. He was so close . . . All he had to do was touch her; no one would ever know . . .

She forced herself to speak. 'Why come to me now?' she asked. 'You've had this eight years. You've obviously known where I am for quite some time. Why wait until now, when I've got so much to lose?'

'I thought I could live without you. I thought that the memory of you, and the film of you, would be enough to sustain me for the rest of my life. I can still get hard just by conjuring up the image of you naked. After all these years. I saw you on television, in magazines, and thought that I could bear to see you with Pierre. But over the years, it got worse, not better. I simply realised that I had to have you again, in the flesh.' He toyed with his frayed cuffs as he spoke and suddenly it seemed obvious.

'Do you need money?' Alice asked. She could see she had genuinely offended him. He looked absolutely brokenhearted and she realised at once that money was not Jacques' object.

'I told you,' he said. 'It's you I want. And I know how concerned you are about your public image, that you would never jeopardise your career by returning to me, so I figured the only way to get what I want from you is blackmail. You won't like it at first, you'll feel guilty, but I'll get you back. I'm sorry it has to be this way, but you'll thank me for it in time, I promise you.'

He paused, and showed her the final photograph in his series. It was all four of the bodies entwined, and although it was hard to distinguish whose limb was whose, there was no mistaking Alice's face, the face that was seen on the cover of a hundred magazines but never like this, blurred, her face smudged not just from the poor picture quality but also by the ecstasy that she was quite clearly feeling. How she longed to feel like that again.

Then Jacques' hands were under the table and when he slid his hand between her legs, using his right hand to hook her panties to one side, she let him. He placed his left thumb directly on to her clitoris. There was no need for him to move the digit. She was aroused enough for simply the feel of his flesh on her pussy after all these years to bring her to an orgasm that sent wave after wave of pleasure through her body. She bit down on her lip, letting pleasure and shame and relief engulf her.

She was still feeling the after-shock convulsions of her orgasm when Jacques swiftly gathered up the pictures and stood up to leave. He held the pictures over his cock to disguise the hard-on she knew must be there. It must have taken all his reserves of self-control to walk away from her, when he knew what she could do with him.

'Now,' said Jacques, 'I think we let the game begin. These are the rules. If you want me to keep your little secret and preserve your career then you have to do exactly what I say. I have many pleasures in mind for you. I would say that the pleasure will be all mine, but I think you'll be getting plenty of pleasure out of the scenarios yourself. If you let yourself. I'll be in touch.' And he walked away, leaving Alice flushed and confused, alone in the café. And the big question buzzed round and around her head. Did blackmailing somebody count when the thing they were forcing you to do was the thing you most desired in the world?

CHAPTER SEVEN

Alice could not sleep. Pierre snored lightly beside her, his arm flung out across the bed, reaching for his wife. He seemed huge, his arms like great hams and his legs like giant logs. But as Alice tossed and turned, her own arms and legs tangled in the Egyptian cotton bedclothes, she could only picture Jacques' wiry frame and felt guilty as she wished Pierre could somehow become Jacques and put out the fire that burned inside her.

Alice was wild with life and lust, and all of her senses seemed sharper than usual. Even her eyesight seemed to have improved in the last few days. In the blue light of night, she could see every detail of her sleeping husband's face. She could smell the day's perfume that lingered around her neck and wrists, taste salty sweat on her lips, and every millimetre of her skin was supersensitive to each touch and caress of the bedclothes. And then what was that noise? A thud and a scratching sound . . . Alice was used to street noises drifting up to her fifth-floor window, but this sounded like it was coming from the end of the corridor, within the building. Could a cat have somehow got inside the apartment? God forbid, a rat? Thoughts of Jacques were replaced by fear that a rodent could be scurrying around in her kitchen. She decided to investigate.

Naked, Alice walked through the double doors that divided her bedroom from the rest of the apartment. Her bare feet made almost no sound on the cold stone floor and she stopped dead in the corridor; there was that sound again. A rustling, or scraping as though a small animal was in the house. It was definitely a rat. She shivered. She would have to wake Pierre; there was no way she could cope with this on her own.

But then she heard a footfall heavier than any animal's. She noticed Jacques' unmistakable smell a fraction of a second before a dark figure stepped out of the bathroom doorway. His hand reached out and grabbed her by the mouth, wrapped an arm around her waist and pulled her into the bathroom. All Alice was aware of was the smell and the feel of him, the buttery softness of his leather jacket, the rough denim of his jeans as he spun her round, and then the lock of his hair as he bent down so that his eyes were level with hers. Alice was aware of her nakedness and how vulnerable and terrified she should be feeling. But she was excited: from nowhere, pressure and tension began to gather between her legs and she felt herself getting wet. She sucked the flesh of his fingers, wanting to taste him. He gently drew his hand away from her mouth and placed it on her collar-bone.

'How did you break into my apartment? How *dare* you? How do you know I won't scream the house down?' Despite her desire, she had to say something to Jacques, otherwise she knew she would hand over control to him completely.

'I know you won't. I know you.' Alice's knees began to quiver. Desire, panic and excitement made her weak.

'Please.' Alice did not want to beg Jacques but she knew that she would have to. 'Does it have to be like this? With my husband asleep in the next room? My career, my marriage . . . If what we had meant anything to you, you wouldn't be doing this to me.'

'What we had meant *everything* to me,' snarled Jacques in a whisper. 'But you lost your right to use that against me when you betrayed me by stealing the film.'

She nodded, fighting back tears.

'OK,' she whispered. 'I'll do whatever you want. We'll meet tomorrow to discuss it. But you need to get out of my house.'

Jacques released his grip on Alice's neck. Relief and disappointment competed for first place in her emotions. She wanted him gone, and yet she wanted him to stay and finish what he'd started. He trailed the old familiar hand down her collar-bone and further down her body, tantalisingly slowly, until he was cupping her breast with the palm of his right hand and idly using his thumb to trace circles around her nipple and watching it grow harder. Alice felt a direct link between his thumb on her nipple and the wetness between her legs. Her left breast was also becoming engorged with blood and silently it begged for his attention. As ever, Jacques read her mind through her body and touched her left nipple, holding his hand motionless on her skin. The stillness of his hands on her tits was a stark contrast to the blood that rushed around her body and the pulse that flickered and throbbed on the tip of her clitoris. He took her nipples between his thumb and forefingers and gently pulled at her breasts, stretching the flesh of her tiny tits away from her body before letting them go. They bounced back to their perky state, making tiny slapping noises.

'I'm not going anywhere,' he breezed softly into her ear, his voice a warm zephyr that caressed her as delicately as any feather. 'Except maybe into your bedroom.'

She shook her head violently but Jacques grabbed her by the neck and marched towards the bedroom. Terror struck her dumb. Not here, not like this. Pierre was older than Jacques but he was bigger and stronger and probably healthier. He would not know who Jacques was.

Thinking him an intruder and a potential rapist, Pierre would probably kill him.

When they were standing outside the bedroom door, Pierre's sleeping form just visible through the curtain, Jacques stood behind Alice with his arm slung around her neck. Alice had no idea what was coming next. His free hand was flat against her stomach. He used his palm to massage her belly in soft circular motions, working his way down towards her bush tantalisingly slowly. When he reached her pubic hair and found it neatly groomed, the skin around it smooth as a peach, he made a tiny murmur of approval in Alice's ear, and then took her ear lobe between his teeth, tugging gently and lightly flicking it with his tongue. Alice bit down hard on her lower lip to stop herself from crying out.

Jacques stroked her bush for a few moments before sliding his middle finger between her pussy lips and finding her damp, swollen clit. Alice longed for him to stimulate it, but his fingertip travelled swiftly over her excited little knob and found her twitching hole. He plunged his finger inside her before removing it and using Alice's juices to massage her clitoris. He simply held his index finger against her clit, feeling her flesh respond to the alchemy of his touch, pressing lightly, and a little harder, and harder still, his fingers moving mere millimetres as he explored the intimate topography of her body. Just as she thought she was about to come, Jacques pushed Alice's head down so that she was bent double. The chink as he undid his belt was almost inaudible but Alice knew what was coming next. She parted her legs and raised herself on to her tiptoes, her gaping pussy inviting Jacques' prick. And then he was inside her, driving it into her. It was still the perfect fit, and Alice found herself shivering and trembling as he began the smooth, rhythmic strokes that stimulated her G-spot. Alice's upper body was limp, tits banging against her knees as he pounded her cunt time and again.

If Pierre had opened his eyes he would have seen the silhouetted figure of his wife bent double, cramming her own fist in her mouth to stifle her groans of ecstasy as another man held her by the hips and plunged a hard cock into her over and over again. He would have seen her freeze for a moment as the orgasm sent her body into a delicious spasm, and he would have seen Jacques' back arch as he came, too.

'This is what I wanted,' whispered Jacques as his balls rose up and emptied themselves into Alice. 'Not money. You. All I've ever wanted is you.' He pulled himself out of her hole and delivered a merciless slap to her tender clitoris before walking away, so light on his feet that the only sound he made was a soft bump as he climbed back the way he had come, through the kitchen window and down the fire escape.

Alice spread out her arms and legs and lay on her back on her bedroom floor, mind reeling, body helpless, like a starfish washed up on the shore.

CHAPTER EIGHT

Jacques next made contact via a letter tucked into some railings directly opposite Alice's beauty therapist. She emerged into the street after her bikini wax and her eyes were immediately drawn to the innocent-looking square of pale blue paper neatly folded between two iron railings. He must have watched her go in, and she wondered if he knew what she had had done to her in there: the hot wax that dripped on to her pussy lips, with a sting that was as pleasurable as it was painful, smeared around her arse, going tantalisingly close to the clitoral hood, then being mercilessly ripped off, leaving her most private and sensitive areas exposed to the uninterested gaze of the beautician, her whole pussy denuded apart from that central downy blonde landing strip of hair on her pubic bone. And the skin, although pink and stinging now, would remain baby-soft and sensitive to Jacques' touch when next they met. With no hair down there, not a drop of wetness was wasted. At any given time, someone could see exactly how turned on you were.

This time, Alice did not wait until she got home but recklessly tore open the envelope in the street, stuffing it into her handbag and opening the letter in full view of anyone who might be watching: fans, paparazzi – she was beginning to care less and less about whether she got caught and more and more about her next adventure. Ironic, really, as the whole reason for having these adventures with Jacques was to protect her reputation, and her own behaviour was growing riskier all the time.

You will walk up and down Rue des Mauvais Garçons until I collect you. Begin at nine tomorrow evening.

The street was in a district she had never visited on foot before, but sometimes glimpsed through the window of chauffeur-driven cars between appointments in more glamorous areas of the city. Often the drivers would apologise before taking her through this tiny cobbled network of alleyways, reassuring her that it was one of the few short-cuts that could beat the Paris traffic in rush-hour. She remembered her naiveté when she had wondered aloud to the driver why there were so many tall women so extravagantly dressed walking down this particular street. He had informed her that these women were in fact trans-sexual prostitutes. Alice had kicked herself for not realising sooner: had life with Pierre made her blind to the vast spectrum of sexuality that thronged the streets outside the walls of their apartment? There were women dressed as men, men dressed as women, a few exotic creatures who could have been either sex; there were people of every race, every colour and every body type. She had marvelled at the sheer variety of what turned people on.

On one such drive, hidden from the sleaze in the street by the dark tinted windows of her limousine, she had seen a woman so like Julie that she had cried out with shock and the driver had screeched to a halt. When the girl was directly outside the window, Alice saw it was not Julie. This girl was younger, her skin even lusher and creamier than Julie's had been, hair redder, curlier and thicker. But her body boasted the same dramatically feminine contours, curves which Alice had a sudden desire to explore, feel and caress. For a crazy second she thought about hiring the girl. She could make an excuse to the driver. After all, what was that window between the client and the driver for if not for closing to create a private space on the back seat of the limousine? But in the time it took for Alice to contemplate peeling the skintight clothes off the girl's body, to find out whether those skimpy shorts that were tight enough to highlight the slit between her legs were leather or rubber or PVC, the driver had put his foot down and accelerated away and the moment was lost for ever.

To keep her appointment with Jacques, Alice did not

travel in a chauffeured limousine but an anonymous taxi, hired on the streets, wearing a crude disguise of a Hermès scarf that she wrapped around her head to ensure that not a strand of her trademark blonde hair was visible and dark glasses that obscured her distinctive grey eyes. She also wore her pale grey trenchcoat, belted in the middle and underneath a simple wool dress.

They turned a corner into a narrow street lined with flickering neon signs and women of all shapes and sizes and she knew that she had reached her destination and some kind of destiny, too. Handsomely tipping the cab driver, she extended one foot out of the car, then the other, swinging her pelvis round and keeping her knees together. Even when she was in disguise, Alice's media training was so ingrained that she emerged from a taxi into a sleazy street as elegantly as she climbed out of a town car on to a red carpet. She caught sight of herself in a sex-shop window, her reflection a translucent ghost projected on to the window that displayed hundreds of pornographic DVD covers. She had to laugh at herself. The scarf, the glasses, the Grace Kelly trenchcoat; she couldn't have looked more like a famous person desperate to avoid recognition if she had tried.

True to her brief, Alice began to walk up and down the small streets. She felt like a sparrow hopping alongside exotic birds of paradise. Despite her dark glasses, she could see perfectly because of the neon signs which broke up the darkness of the narrow street. She was so transfixed by the other women that she almost forgot to look out for Jacques.

She saw him loitering in the doorway of one of the smaller shops. The flickering pink sign spelled out the words Miss Demeanour and it was one of the more female-friendly shops along the street, with erotic lingerie as well as DVDs in the window. He wore a tight-fitting suit which showed off his slim frame and a black shirt and tie. He looks like a pimp, thought Alice, and instantly realised the nature of the game he would play with her tonight. Trepidation and excitement flowed through her.

Wordlessly Alice followed him inside. He did not speak to her, and she did not dare to say anything for fear that someone would recognise her distinctive voice. Jacques proceeded to go shopping, picking garments off the shelves and rails seemingly at random. He selected white PVC boots that came all the way up to her thighs and a pink dress made of clinging Lycra. It had cutaways at the side and the midsection of the dress consisted of slinky silver chainmail. It was made of flimsy fabric and once on would leave nothing to the imagination. Alice noticed that Jacques walked past the lingerie section without stopping to pick up a bra or any panties. Finally he picked up a long, black wig. The thick tumbling tresses were as unlike Alice's own fine shoulder-length natural blonde hair as could be. She noted with some relief that the wig also had a thick black fringe which would fall across her eyes and help to further obscure her identity. Jacques paid for the items while Alice pretended to be interested in some of the more tame underwear, demure white lace obviously intended for a wedding night.

Jacques muttered something to the sales assistant, who nodded, and the next thing she knew, Alice was being ushered into the tiny cubicle. Jacques drew the fraying red velvet curtain closed.

'Strip' he commanded. Alice disrobed slowly, aware that her body would betray the arousal she felt simply at being so close to Jacques. Her nipples were hot and rock hard and the tops of her thighs were glistening with the gossamer dew that always accompanied his presence. She handed over to Jacques the simple city dress and kitten-heeled slingbacks she had been wearing and in exchange she received the cheap, tacky outfit that he had selected for her.

'Seeing you dress like a cheap whore is going to get me harder than I've ever been in my life,' snarled Jacques. 'The mighty Alice Daumier, dressed up like a cheap tart. Reduced to a street-walker.'

As he spoke he manhandled Alice's body, raising her arms above her head, and cruelly forcing the skimpy pink dress over her head so that the silvery chainmail scratched her soft skin. There was even less fabric than she had thought and barely enough to cover her nipples. The sides of her breasts were exposed, the soft curve of flesh even paler than the rest of her milky body. The skirt was so short that the crease where the top of her thigh met her arse was visible if she bent down even an inch or two.

'Please,' begged Alice, 'Please, Jacques, at least allow me the dignity of some underwear.'

'You still don't get it, do you?' he said, amused. 'This is all about removing your dignity. I'm going to debase you, Alice. Strip away everything you've built up since you left me. You're complaining, but your body tells another story. You're as horny as I am. Don't bother denying it, I can smell it on you.'

He knelt before her and helped her into the white boots. The five-inch heels tipped Alice's whole body forwards so that she could not have run away even if she had had the courage to. Then Jacques put the wig on her and from his pocket, produced a hot pink frosted lipstick, so lurid and nasty that only a whore advertising her mouth as a receptacle for cock would ever paint her lips with it. It was certainly a far cry from Alice's usual make-up palette of subtle roses and nude shades. After Jacques had tenderly applied the lipstick in a cruel, teasing imitation of his kiss, he spun her round and showed her reflection in the tiny changing-room mirror.

'You look like a whore,' whispered Jacques, 'and

tonight, precious Alice, award-winning actress, dutiful wife, you are going to walk the streets and be one.'

She had known it was coming but hearing him say it was still shocking. She, a pampered princess, was about to take her place in a dirty dance with women of the night. She didn't want to do it, but she would cope, for the reflection she saw was not her. She would method act her way through this, assume the identity of the woman in the mirror, that hooker with the long black hair, the second-skin pink dress with its metallic midriff and the street-walker boots.

'Now go,' said Jacques and tucked her handbag under his arm. 'I will look after this. You don't need it, and I want to see the cash from your transaction. I need to know that you really went through with this.' Without her handbag, which contained her phone, her keys and her wallet, it all became real. Suddenly the reality of what she was doing dawned on her. She didn't know much about the kind of man that went to visit prostitutes, but she expected to have to service a procession of unattractive, sleazy, smelly, middle-aged men who would penetrate her, grunting unpleasantly for a few seconds before driving off into the night and returning to their wives. Alice had never been with somebody she didn't find attractive before: could she method act a wet and eager cunt? If she wasn't turned on, would it hurt?

Jacques pushed her out into the street and vanished.

Agonising minutes passed while cars drove slowly past her and passed her over. Alice was acutely aware of the cold night air against her naked pussy and her nipples, hard like two little pebbles, protruding through her slinky dress. Finally, a shiny black Mercedes with tinted windows crawled down the street and somehow Alice knew he was going to hire her. She glanced at the car's number plate and noticed that it was brand new. She might be about to fuck a gross old guy, but at least she would fuck one with money.

The driver's window opened with an almost inaudible hiss and a voice inside asked her how much it would be for straight sex. Alice was relieved that he did not couch his request in the coded language of the streets but immediately realised with a dizzying panic that she had no idea how much to charge. She quoted him 100 euros. The low whistle he let out told her that she had massively overpriced herself and she resigned herself to the fact that he would close the window and drive off into the night before she ever got a proper look at his face.

'You're asking over the odds,' he said, 'but a hard little body like yours is rare on the streets. I bet you've got a nice, tight little cunt to go with those pointy little tits.' Alice heard a peep and the click as he automatically unlocked the back door and she slid into the passenger seat.

'We won't go far,' said the punter. In the dark of the

car interior she could only tell that his hair was dark and short – like every other man in Paris under the age of fifty. He swung his car round to the right and Alice found herself in a dark, abandoned alley behind some back doors of restaurants. There was no light in the alleyway, and when the stranger turned off the ignition key and dimmed the lights inside the car, it was even more impossible to make out the contours of his face. The thought of being screwed by a man without a face was strangely horny to Alice.

One thing Alice did know from having played a part in a movie which featured prostitutes was that sex workers always took their money up front.

'Cash,' she said.

'I was about to pay, don't worry. I've got a feeling you'll be worth it.' They made eye contact in the driver's rear-view mirror. She could only see a pair of black eyes which devoured the very sight of her. His breath grew shallower as he tilted the mirror, allowing his gaze to travel down her body.

'Get in the back,' he said, tilting the driver's seat so that she could climb through the gap. She manoeuvred herself through head-first and felt his breath on the backs of her thighs as she eased herself over the gearstick and on to the seat. For a few seconds what light there was was blocked out as he followed her through and sat close to her, running his hand down the bones of her back.

'I haven't had a skinny bitch like you in a long time,' he said, and she noticed a huskiness and depth to his voice that had been lacking before. He peeled five 20 euro notes out of his wallet and threw them at her one by one. The paper floated to the ground like feathers, caressing her body. She had to kneel on the car floor to pick up every note.

'That's right, stick your pretty arse up in the air while you look for your money. Christ, I'm getting hard just looking at you in that pink dress. Stay on all fours. Don't move. I want to have you from behind.'

There was the sound of a zip being undone and the tear and snap of a condom being removed from its packet and rolled over a hard dick. Then he was stabbing at her arse and thighs with the tip of his erection. He wasn't lying about being hard: it was like being poked with a warm wooden truncheon. The featherlight-thin pink dress was barely there as it was, but when he forced it over her arse, exposing her skin, she felt more thrillingly vulnerable than ever. The chainmail scraped her skin like a violent caress. She was excited, but too nervous to get as wet as she needed to be to accommodate a hard-on that substantial. But it didn't seem to matter to the man. He inserted a warm thumb into her hole, which was only damp, not dripping.

'Don't worry,' he breathed, 'I've met dirty bitches like

you before. Your hobby is your job. You're gonna love this just as much as I will.'

He was inside her before he had finished speaking, spreading her unwilling pussy and forcing a prick thicker than she had expected inside her. He mistook Alice's wince of discomfort for pleasure and thrust into her, hard. As he pounded away at her, to her surprise discomfort turned to a vague warm pleasure. Just as she was beginning to rock her hips in time to the rhythm of his thrusts, he pulled out of her.

'Turn over,' he said. 'Get your tits out.'

Alice rolled on to her back and spread her legs wide, letting him see the pussy that was now swollen and glistening in the half-light. She pulled the dress down so that her small breasts were exposed. He put his hands on them and massaged her nipples. Alice felt the electricity of his touch in her clit as well as her breasts and longed for him to stimulate her there, but knew he was not paying her to please herself. This time when he penetrated her she was ready and greedy for cock, wrapping her feet around his waist and trying to rub her clit against his pubic hair, desperate for the stimulation that would bring her to orgasm with this unlikely partner. But when he suddenly became still and shuddered and swore before going limp, she knew that it wasn't going to happen. She had gone from unwilling whore to the brink of an orgasm in the space of a few minutes, and although Alice was relieved she had risen to Jacques' challenge, she couldn't help feel cheated and disappointed.

The client pulled out of her and rolled the condom off his subsiding erection. Alice closed her legs, wishing he would leave her alone for just a few seconds so that she could use her own skilled hands to give her her own orgasm, but instead he was zipping himself up and crawling back through to the front. I will never know what he looks like, thought Alice, as he unlocked the passenger door. Alice made sure that her nipples and pussy were covered by her slip of a dress and left him in his car. He reversed out of the alleyway and was gone in seconds, leaving Alice on her own in a strange back street with a pounding clit, a spinning head and 100 euros in cash tucked into her white boot.

Staggering back on to the main street, Alice bumped into another girl, and caught her breath. It was the girl, she was sure of it. The one who looked like Julie but was not Julie. She did not realise she was staring until the girl walked up to her and challenged her.

'This is my bit of the street,' she said. Her accent was educated Parisian and her voice soft and sexy. An idea came to Alice and she acted on the impulse before she had a chance to change her mind.

'I'm not working,' said Alice. 'I'm buying. I want you.'

'You?' The girl looked Alice up and down. 'Are you mad?'

'I think I probably am,' conceded Alice. 'But you remind me of someone I used to know.'

'OK,' said the girl, still looking at Alice as though she were insane, then threw back her head and laughed. 'What the hell. To be honest, it will probably make a nice change from servicing fat, ugly, married men.'

Alice was quaking with fear and anticipation as she followed the girl down another tiny cobbled back street and into a dark doorway, which gave on to a dark red-painted stairway lit with a string of fairy lights. Alice followed the girl up the stairs, taking care not to trip on the tattered carpet, still unsure of her tread in these ridiculous heels. As she did, she got a great back view of the hooker. The skin-tight leather hotpants she wore left nothing to the imagination; her arse-crack and the soft swell of her round buttocks were inches away from Alice's face and the fishnet stockings she wore underneath did little to hide an expanse of creamy white thigh. Alice licked her lips as she noticed the tight waistband cutting into the girl's waist and a spillage of full but firm flesh peeking over the top. And then there was that hair; that long, red, spiralling hair, a burnt-orange mass of curls against the pale soft blue of her denim jacket. Alice could tell that the hair was so vividly red as to be dyed. I wonder what colour her bush is, thought Alice. Dark or fair? Is she hairy or shaved or waxed like me? It had been years since Alice had been naked with another woman and she was excited to be recreating the experience with someone who looked so like Julie. But she was excited for another reason, too: she was being bad and disobedient, getting a petty revenge on Jacques by refusing to play his game by his rules. There would be repercussions, she was sure, but she felt wild and mad and rebellious and horny.

The girl's room was lit by a single lamp, over which was strewn a lace scarf, casting a soft dappled shade over the room. The bed, in the middle of the room, was covered in a cheap nylon counterpane. Alice could virtually feel the static electricity crackling just by looking at it. The thought of the expensive, high-thread-count Egyptian cotton sheets on her bed at home reminded her how far removed this girl and her room were from her usual starched, laundered life. The idea thrilled her and made her crave stimulation. Alice could not wait to get naked with the girl. She pressed 50 euros into the girl's hand, money that had been thrown at her naked, crouching body in the back of the car only minutes before. As the girl's eyes widened in appreciation, Alice could tell that she had paid over the odds. She didn't care.

'What's your name?' Alice asked the girl whose room she stood in.

'Sylvie,'

'Well, Sylvie,' said Alice. 'I'd like to see you take your clothes off for me.' It felt so good to be the one giving the orders after having obeyed Jacques' commands for so long. Alice felt like she was reclaiming some of her dignity. Even if Jacques did expose her secret, at least she would always know that she had got one over on him by sneaking this liaison with Sylvie.

Alice watched, transfixed, as Sylvie removed the denim jacket to reveal a pair of splendid globe-shaped breasts, squeezed almost up to her chin by a basque made of red and black satin. As Alice had hoped, the spare flesh on Sylvie's belly spilled out underneath and over the top of the garment. Alice felt her pussy, so recently pounded by a stranger's cock, begin to swell and lift, and knew that her orgasm, when it came, was going to be one of the sweetest and strongest she'd ever had.

'Here,' said Alice, as Sylvie began to unlace her corset. 'Let me help you with that.' Inches away from the prostitute, Alice tugged at the thin black ribbon which held the boned fabric together. Faster than she had expected, the top fell open at the front, revealing her breasts, extremely firm for their size. Round, large, dark pinky-brown nipples pointed slightly upwards and, as Alice took a breast in each hand, she was delighted and gratified to see that they began to stiffen and protrude. Alice had never seen another pair of tits react like this. Sylvie's nipples grew and grew until they were at least an inch long, sticking out like clothes pegs. Their tawny colour indicated that Sylvie would have a dark bush. She was not like Julie, fair and rosy and freckled, but olive-skinned.

Alice felt her own breasts respond in kind, and moaned with delight when Sylvie caressed her shoulders and gently pulled down the Lycra straps that held her own pink clingy dress in place. The two women were now inches apart, both topless. It was hard to say who moved towards whom as they pressed themselves together and began to kiss. Sylvie's full lips were so soft that Alice felt as though she were kissing a flower. The soft velvety petals parted to reveal and welcome her into a large, sweet-tasting mouth and a probing tongue which explored Alice's own mouth languidly at first. As the two women's breasts rubbed together, Alice's puffy nipples colliding with Sylvie's bullet-shaped ones, the kiss became more urgent. Sylvie raised a hand to run her fingers through Alice's hair. In the nick of time, Alice remembered that she was wearing a long black wig. Abruptly she snatched Sylvie's hand and, because she wanted it there as well as to distract her attention from her hair, placed it on her hip, hoping that Sylvie would follow her lead and peel down her skirt.

Sylvie pulled away, and Alice was thrilled to see that the girl's innocent-looking face had been smeared with her own hot-pink whore's lipstick, on her lips and all over her cheeks where their mouths had clashed in a tournament of tongues.

'God, this is horny,' breathed Sylvie as Alice slowly slid her hands into the waistband of her hotpants. '*You're* horny. Let me tell you, you're making me wetter than any male client has for a long, long time.' Alice was delirious with lust now, and Sylvie's words only further stoked the fire burning in her pussy. She dropped to her knees, the over-the-knee white boots providing a barrier between her skin and the carpeted floor. She wanted her first glimpse of Sylvie's bush to be at eye level, and she wanted to know just how wet the girl was. She unfastened the first button of Sylvie's shorts and was delighted by the little pink marks the tight clothes had made on her skin, and by the over-spill of her voluptuous flesh when it was liberated. Alice kissed the skin below Sylvie's navel, greedily sucking at the flesh, leaving a hot pink lipstick smear on the flawless skin. She could smell Sylvie's pussy, the musk of her arousal intensified by a cunt encased in tight leather hotpants.

Alice leaned back and Sylvie stretched her arms over her head, lifting those stupendous breasts so that Alice could admire their undersides. With one swift movement, Alice pulled down Sylvie's shorts, bringing the fishnet tights down too so that they were puddled around her ankles. Sylvie's muff was a dark brown, luxuriant triangle but she parted her dewy thighs to reveal that her pussy lips and arsehole were waxed as bare as Alice's own cunt. Alice buried her face in Sylvie's soft, glossy pubic hair, before letting her tongue part the top of her pussy and push back the clitoral hood. The bead of flesh which her tongue exposed was erect and pulsating like a mini-penis. Funny how you never forget how to do some things, Alice thought, as she administered a series of featherlight flicks to Sylvie's clit, simultaneously hitching her pink and metallic dress up around her own waist, and touching herself between her legs, sliding her middle finger deep inside her cunt to lubricate it before furiously rubbing her own pulsating clitoris.

Sylvie's knees began to quiver and she dropped to the floor, pulling Alice down to the carpet with her. Alice was momentarily distracted by a book that lay open and face down by the side of the bed. It was an acting book, one that she had studied herself while she was at drama school. This glimpse into the world of a really struggling actress made Alice grateful that she had never known what it was like to be out of work. She felt a momentary surge of guilt at her own good fortune and was reminded that Pierre had helped to make her career, and here she was betraying him by fucking another woman in a back street of Paris. But as Sylvie leaned over her and let a stiff brown nipple dangle tantalisingly close to Alice's lips, she realised there was no time for guilt, only for hot, horny passion. She wrapped her mouth around the other woman's breast and sucked, greedily.

The two women began to roll together on the shiny carpet, their pussies rubbing together, swelling and moistening all the while until it was impossible to tell whose juice was whose. They kissed greedily, allowing their breasts to clash and become entangled, rolling over and over and over together so that one minute Alice was on top, bearing down on Sylvie with all her weight, while the next minute Sylvie would be on top, grinding down into Alice's body and threatening to suffocate her. They clawed at each other's bodies, grabbed each other's breasts and shook and jiggled them, delighting in their differences. Alice propped herself up on her forearms and dangled a breast over Sylvie's mouth. Sylvie took her cue and placed the whole of her soft, voluptuous mouth around the tiny breast. With her free hand she flattened her palm and began to rub Alice's vulva in a smooth, flat motion that created just enough friction to bring Alice to the edge of orgasm. Then she broke away, and turned her body around so that she was underneath Alice with her head at her feet in a 69 position.

Mouths on each other's cunts, both women delved voraciously. Sylvie tasted as good as she smelled, and Alice could feel her clit erect and sensitive, growing harder as she licked it and teased it with the tip of her nose. She moaned underneath Alice and the two women fell into a perfect rhythm, rocking, sucking, bucking together. Alice knew that Sylvie was about to come because her body tensed and she sucked at Alice's clit as though drinking milk from a teat. Alice felt the rapid contractions of Sylvie's pussy on her mouth as she surrendered to the orgasm. Sylvie let out a low moan of pleasure before saying, 'I'm coming hard, I'm coming, I'm coming . . .'

Alice followed suit, the tension that had been building in her body finally exploding, allowing herself to collapse on the soft bed of Sylvie's belly. The two women lay like this for a few seconds, both spent by their orgasms, occasionally planting cooling kisses on each other's clits. Alice felt Sylvie's warm breath caressing her satiated pussy and arsehole, and when she saw liquid silk pooling out of Sylvie's pussy, she could not resist licking it from the swollen, dark red flesh.

'That's the best 50 euros I've ever spent,' Alice mumbled into Sylvie's damp bush.

'It's certainly the best 50 euros I've ever earned,' replied the satisfied whore.

The relaxed atmosphere in the room vanished with the click of the door opening. Alice felt Sylvie's body stiffen.

'Who the fuck are you? How did you get into my

room?' Alice did not share Sylvie's panic, although she felt terribly exposed with her spread pussy and arsehole, still dripping and swollen, pointed towards the open door. She could not see the intruder from her position, but she knew who it was.

'It's cool, Sylvie, he's come for me,' said Alice, raising herself to a crouching position and turning to face Jacques. Sylvie gathered the scarf that had been draped over the lamp, and gathered it about herself to cover her body. After her orgasm, her cheeks were flushed and her eyes bright. Her hair tumbled over dimpled shoulders, making her look like a figure from a Renaissance painting. Alice sat on the floor with her knees on one side.

'You've cheated.' Jacques' voice was harsh. 'The deal was that you fucked one man and gave me the money. But you ran away from me again. I knew you would. I followed the car round to the alleyway, and listened to the sound of him fucking you. I looked in the window and saw you spread your arse while he stuck it in you. God, you fucking loved it. I stood there with my dick in my hand, getting harder and harder by the second.' Jacques took a step towards Alice where she lay trembling, and went to pull her up by the hair. The wig came off in his hand. As Alice's own fair hair tumbled about her shoulders, she was instantly recognisable. Sylvie gasped in disbelief as Jacques continued to talk.

'It's appropriate that I made you act the whore. After all, that's what you've been doing with your husband all this time, isn't it? Sleeping your way to the top? Don't look at me like that. I know he can't do to you what I can. It came so naturally to you in the back of that car . . . you got so horny you had to go and get a bit of pussy. I didn't say you could do that, and I'll think of a way to punish you later. But for now,' he leered, his hand going to his crotch, 'I think the least you can do is help me to get rid of this hard-on.'

He held Alice by her real hair this time, roughly forcing her around and on to her knees. His dick was out of his trousers and in her face before she had time to protest: the tip of it was bashing against her oesophagus, making her gag, but tasting so good and feeling so right she grabbed his arse and pushed it deeper down her throat. He rammed his dick as hard as he could, causing whiplash in her neck, fucking her face mercilessly. Her tits brushed against his knees and his balls slapped against her chin.

'Taste it, you greedy little bitch.' Alice made muffled moans of satisfaction, and was astonished once more to feel herself becoming aroused, her aching pussy which had so recently been pounded by a stranger's cock and sucked to orgasm becoming damp again. She wasn't the only one ready for round two: she became aware of Sylvie on the bed behind them and letting her scarf fall from her body, crawling closer to the couple, squeezing and massaging her breasts and licking her lips. The sight of voluptuous Sylvie getting off was too much for Jacques and he came with an animal yowl. Hot salty spunk cascaded over Alice's face, stinging her eyes and filling up her nose and mouth, dribbling down her chest. She lapped it up hungrily and so did Sylvie, sucking the cream out of the little hollow at the base of Alice's neck, wrapping her tongue around the skinny girl's collar-bone. Sylvie worked her way up Alice's neck, laving her with her tongue like a cat, until their lips were touching. Greedily, Sylvie drank the spunk from Alice's mouth, tongue travelling over teeth, not wanting to waste a drop. As they pulled apart, their mouths remained joined by a trickle of semen, a thin elastic strand of liquid which eventually broke in two, and landed with a slap on Sylvie's tits. Alice gently and tenderly massaged the milky balm into the other woman's full breasts. Jacques observed this tender scene with apparent disinterest, shaking his dick and flicking the remaining drops of cum in their direction. Tiny beads of it decorated the curls of Sylvie's hair like jewels. Jacques kicked the bag containing Alice's clothes and handbag into the centre of the room, tucked his dick into his jeans and left without a word or a backward glance. Silence filled the room.

'Well,' said Sylvie. 'I don't know about you, but I need a smoke.' She reached into her bedside drawer, her round breasts falling to one side as she pulled out a packet of cigarettes and a lighter. Alice gratefully took the cigarette that was offered to her, the nicotine rush enhancing her post-orgasmic, blissed-out state.

'I don't believe it. Alice Daumier. In my apartment. On my face!' It was so bizarre that Sylvie began to giggle. Her laughter was so warm that Alice couldn't help but join in. 'What the fucking hell are you doing here?'

What was the point of lying? Sylvie would probably be on the phone to the press the second she left the door. If she was going to be exposed, they might as well get the story straight.

'He's an ex. *The* ex,' she said, and Sylvie nodded, understanding. 'He's got some dirt on me from years ago, before I was famous. If it gets out, my career's over and so's my marriage. He's blackmailing me, I suppose, putting me through all these little tests, making me play his sex games, dancing to his tune. I'm completely at his mercy. And then I saw you there, and you looked so horny, I just wanted to do something spontaneous, for myself.'

'There's more to it than that,' said Sylvie, producing a bottle of brandy from her bedside drawer and offering the bottle to Alice before taking a swig herself. 'I've seen the way you were sucking his dick. You enjoyed it just as much as he did.'

What is my life coming to, thought Alice, when I am

naked, getting drunk with a whore in this awful part of town? I barely recognise the way I am behaving. But she felt comfortable in Sylvie's presence. As the clock struck one, Alice realised it was time to go. Sylvie would need to get back to work.

'I should go,' she said, and then, awkwardly, 'I've taken up so much of your time tonight. Keep the other 50 euros.'

'I wouldn't have gone back on the street tonight anyway,' replied Sylvie. 'What happened between us tonight was so delicious I couldn't bear to take a regular client.' Then confusion and hurt clouded her features. 'I don't want money for silence or anything, you know. You can trust me.' Alice looked at the round, honest eyes and believed her.

'Although there's one thing I'd like.' Alice's heart sank. Here comes the blackmail.

'What?'

'I'd love to keep this pink dress and these boots.'

Alice smiled with relief.

'They're yours,' she said, and paused to imagine Sylvie in the hot pink dress with the cutaway sides, flesh spilling over the side and the chainmail scratching her, her smooth milky thighs spilling over the tops of the boots. 'On one condition. You can't try them on now. You'd look so horny in them that I'd probably have to fuck you all over again and quite frankly I need to go home, calm down, have a shower, go to bed and get my head around all this. I think if I have another orgasm tonight I might actually die of pleasure.'

Sylvie threw back her head and roared a throaty, sexy laugh.

'It's a deal,' she replied. 'If you ever want to hang out here again, you know where to find me.' She wrote her number on a slip of paper.

The two women exchanged a long, lingering kiss goodbye. Sylvie's mouth tasted of brandy, cigarettes, spunk and Alice's own pussy.

Dressed in the clothes she had left the house in, Alice wrapped the scarf around her head, went out on to the street and hailed a cab. As the rainy streets flew past the window, the seedy district gradually transformed itself into her own chic neighbourhood. She thought about what Sylvie had said. Was she going along with Jacques' games because she was scared of being exposed, or because she was addicted to him? The truth scared and aroused her.

CHAPTER NINE

Alice came home from her big audition in a bad mood. This thing with Jacques was completely jangling her nerves, and she had fluffed her lines and not been able to fake chemistry with her potential new co-star. What a waste of a 400 euro dress, she thought, looking down at the black knee-length outfit she had invested in specifically for the audition. It sculpted her figure into an hourglass shape, but it had not worked its magic today. Soon, thought Alice, Jacques might expose me and I will never be able to afford a dress like this again. Is it even worth going to auditions any more? Will I ever be able to concentrate on acting again? I don't even have Jacques' guarantee that when he has finished playing his games with me he will leave me alone and that I will have the tape in my possession.

Alice was too tired to take the stairs. She pushed the button that summoned the elevator with a heavy heart, looking forward to a long bath when she was in her apartment. The lift rattled down through the floors, and when the cage arrived at the ground floor, Alice nearly fainted with shock to see Jacques peering at her through the mesh. He looked more rugged than ever; his crumpled clothes and dirty face thrown into starker relief than usual by the grand imposing marble staircase and the filigree ironwork of the lift and banisters. He wore a long, black leather coat with fraying and dirty patches which came down to his ankles and engulfed his body, giving him an air of mystery and menace. He pulled open the metal trellis gate, grabbed Alice's waist, forced her into the lift and shut the door behind them. It was not a big space, perhaps two metres square, and despite the fact that she could see through the walls, she suddenly felt very claustrophobic. Her breath began to grow sharp and shallow. Jacques pressed a button and the lift began its noisy ascent.

Jacques pulled a length of black, shiny material out of an inside coat pocket. Alice's heart soared. It looked like videotape and Alice thought for one thrilling second that he had decided to give her the film and that she was free of him. He has forgiven me, she thought. I'm free. My career, my world, it's all going to be all right.

But her hopes were dashed as soon as they rose. For it soon became apparent that it was not videotape at all but another kind of tape, stronger, stickier and thicker than the flimsy vinyl ribbon of a video cassette. Suddenly Jacques was kissing her, holding her arms at the wrist and pressing them out to the side and above her head so that she felt crucified. The intensity of his kiss distracted her from the fact that he was deftly binding her hands to the bars of the inside of the lift with the tape. Because of the din the lift made, Alice could not hear if there were people coming and going on any of the landings, but she knew that all it would take would be for one resident to see her like this and the whole game would be up. This was the riskiest game yet. And on her home ground, too.

Jacques took a step back, kept his hands around Alice's waist and tugged her to make sure she was securely bound. The tape was sticky as well as tight and it tore at the tiny hairs on her wrists as she tried to free herself. But another thought occurred to Alice as she struggled: now that he has me prisoner, now that I can't run away, I can abandon myself to whatever he wants. I have no option but to surrender my body to him.

Jacques' hands travelled down Alice's body, smoothing down the stiff brushed cotton of her dress, this stroking a cruel shadow of the skin-on-skin contact she craved. He knelt before her and reached up the material of her skirt, hands massaging her legs. A snag in his nail tore her stockings. He bit the lacy top of the stocking, nipping the dewy skin of Alice's inner thigh with merciless teeth. He buried his face between those thighs and inhaled deeply. He had his thumbs under the sides of her panties and pulled them down over her feet although he left her shoes, her laddered stockings and her suspender belt on. Using the remainder of the tape, Jacques forced Alice's legs apart as far as they could go. No yoga lesson or dance class could have prepared her for the pain she felt as her inner thighs were stretched in opposite directions. Now her pussy, clit and arsehole were uncovered and in full view. She was in an X-shape tied to the wall, bound, exposed and absolutely helpless.

After tugging at each of the restraints to make sure she was secure, and sending a delicious frisson through her body every time he did so, Jacques held Alice's panties over his face and breathed in deeply before stuffing them under her nose, rubbing the gusset under her nostrils, forcing her to breathe in the sweet, musky juice that betrayed how excited he was making her. Then, finally, he spoke.

'I do believe you're enjoying this as much as I am,' he said, thoughtfully. 'Let's see how you enjoy it when I crank things up a notch.' He opened his coat, stuffing the panties into his inside pocket and at the same time removing a pair of silver dressmaker's scissors. Holding the blades in his hand, he placed the handle against her hot, steaming pussy. The coldness of the steel was delicious, and Alice thought that if he would only use the smooth, curved handles to stimulate her clit, she could come there and then and get the release her body and mind craved. But of course Jacques would not gratify her that quickly or easily. He inserted the side of the handle a millimetre or so into her pussy. The cool metal slithered between her slippery lips and she realised just how wet she was. And how hot she was between her legs, too; the shock of the cold steel diminished as it warmed to her body temperature.

Jacques then removed the scissors and licked them clean, leaning in to kiss her so that she could taste her own pussy juices and the metallic tang of the scissors on his lips and tongue. His tongue exploring her teeth made her long for his fingers on her clit. Blood pumping between her legs took her mind off the agonising ache in her arms and legs. Her hands were beginning to go numb, and her thighs were starting to shake. And then there was the other feeling that made her shiver. The fear that at any moment, one of her neighbours could leave their luxury apartment and witness the squeaky clean Alice Daumier in the throes of a bondage game with a man who was most definitely not her husband. Thank goodness she was still wearing her dress, even if it was hitched around her waist. At least her tits were still covered.

'What are you going to do with me?'

'I'm going to see you,' said Jacques softly, idly tracing his tongue and teeth over the scissors as though lost in thought and deciding what to do next, although Alice did not doubt that this whole game had been planned for days.

'You can see me now,' said Alice, puzzled.

'I can't see all of you,' replied Jacques, and with a flourish and precision that would have impressed the sternest of Parisian couturiers, he slipped the blade between her legs, tapped her pubic hair with the scissor tip and then parted the blades and sliced through the stiff, starchy fabric as though it were tissue paper. He made a clean cut from hem to neckline so that Alice's expensive dress ceased to cocoon her contours and instead hung loosely about her like an unbuttoned coat. She wore no bra and her tits protruded with engorged, dark pink nipples, like a pair of eyes blinking at sudden and unexpected light. Instead of the tender sucking that her breasts craved, Jacques lightly smacked the underside of each one with the blades of the scissors, watching the fleshy little mounds wobble. Lust flickered in his eyes like a candle that could not be extinguished.

Jacques slashed the rest of the dress, performing two incisions on the front of the sleeves, so that the rest of the fabric fell away. With one swift yank, he pulled the tattered, once-expensive garment away from Alice's body and discarded it on the floor behind him. Alice was now naked and splayed out in an X-shape, the ironwork grille of the lift digging into the skin of her back and her arse. The lift continued to travel up and down the building, passing every floor, Jacques reaching to depress a button and keep it going whenever it approached the ground or

top floors. Surely it was only a matter of time before somebody wondered why the lift was constantly in motion,
stepped out of their apartment to complain about the
noise, or just happened to be walking by on the stairs. By
now Alice had pretty much abandoned herself to the
thought that this was the final act of Jacques' sick games,
and the end of her career and life as she knew it. Unless
she could get him to come, and let her come, and bring
it all to an end soon.

'Jacques . . . please . . .'

'I like to hear that,' said Jacques. 'I like to hear you
beg. Let me see . . . are you about to beg me to suck your
tits? To go down on you? To put my cock in your hole?'

Alice let out a low moan and her pussy throbbed,
aching for his prick. A fresh gush of moisture flooded her
cunt, oozed along her lips and around to her arse and
finally made a little splash on the floor.

'I could fuck you now,' said Jacques. 'God knows,
my dick's hard enough.' With the same sleight of hand
he had used to cut away her dress, he undid his fly and
whipped out that familiar yet thrilling hard-on that made
Alice's mouth, not to mention her pussy, water even more.
'Yes,' he pondered, his hand wandering up and down the
shaft of his cock and pulling back the foreskin to reveal
a globule of pre-cum, a pearly droplet that Alice could
almost taste, 'but this is not about my satisfaction, it's

about teaching you a lesson. And the lesson is not over yet.'

He began to fumble in the depths of his coat again. What the hell else was in there, Alice wondered, as her eyes flitted between his hands exploring his pockets and his dick, twitching and bolt upright even without manual stimulation. He pulled out a tiny object, about the size of a lipstick and shaped like a large bullet. It was made of a shiny plastic, the same azure blue as Jacques' eyes. He held it up, examining it as though it were a precious jewel, and the mysterious object twinkled in the dim light. It was not until he twisted its base, and a faint buzzing noise became audible underneath the crank and clang of the lift mechanism, that Alice realised it was a vibrator. Jacques held it to her neck and ran it down the curves of her body, sending an intense caress that simultaneously stimulated and numbed her skin. Pinching her nipple, he held it to the tip of the tit, giving her pins and needles. Jacques let the breast go, gave it a gentle slap to get the blood flowing back to it and turned his attention to the other one. Alice looked down at her chest. She had never seen her nipples this pink or swollen before, had not known that they could grow to such a size that they were as big as her actual breasts. Just when she thought she could not stand the tingling any more, Jacques took the vibrator away from her tits and ran it up and down the underside of his dick. From the way he was biting his lip, Alice could not tell if he was getting himself harder, or trying to numb himself to make himself last longer. If only he would jab it inside her, he could put both of them out of their misery.

He did the next best thing: he held the toy to her hard, erect clitoris and Alice felt the first waves of pleasure radiate from her pussy that told her orgasm was imminent. Producing another short length of black tape, Jacques bound the vibrating bullet tightly against Alice's clit, winding the black tape around her waist and looping it over one of her thighs. The tape was tight and bit into her flesh. Alice sighed in ecstasy.

'I'm going to come soon. Please. Please. I want you inside me when I do.'

'Are you begging, Alice Daumier?'

'Yes, I'm fucking begging!' she wailed, all pretence of dignity and control abandoned in her desperate need to release the tension. 'I need it. I need your cock. Spear me, fuck me, let me come!'

As she spoke she realised that her words were ringing out for anybody in the vicinity to hear. The lift had stopped. Jacques had pulled the door of the lift open a fraction and forced the lift to a juddering halt between the third and fourth floors. Suddenly the staircase was silent but for Alice's desperate pleas echoing off the walls. She could hear nothing but the sound of her own breathing and the creak of the tape that bound her and the buzzing of the little vibrating bullet that was even now swelling her clit to an almost unbearable state of arousal.

'Keep talking,' he said.

And then another noise. The unmistakable sound of the heavy front door opening and closing with a key, which could only mean that one of the other residents was coming in, and she was about to be seen. But Alice kept talking.

'I'm addicted to your prick, Jacques. It is the only one that's ever felt right inside me,' she whispered. The truth might as well come out now. 'I loved sucking it, I loved you inside me; it's just the best dick in the world.'

'I can't hear you. Louder.'

Footsteps on the stairs told Alice her neighbours were seconds away from turning the corner and seeing her. It was over. Might as well enjoy the moment. Alice's aching body tensed as she summoned what strength she had left and screamed at the top of her lungs, 'I will die if you don't put your dick in me right now! Fuck me, Jacques! Fuck me! You know how good we are together. You need it too. Fuck me! Fuck me! Fuck me!'

But there was no audience for Alice's words, for Jacques had started the lift again the moment she began to shout. As the ancient machinery began its deafening journey upwards to the sixth floor, he finally gave her what she wanted. Hooking his thumbs in between her pussy lips to stretch her opening just that little bit further and looking at the drenched pink hole, he licked his lips and smiled at Alice. There was triumph and cruelty in that smile. Jacques thrust his fat hard-on into Alice's spasming pussy the second she allowed herself to surrender to the vibrations on her clitoris. She had a whole-body orgasm, the contractions in her pussy massaging his dick and her arms and legs shaking uncontrollably. Jacques penetrated her as she came, his prick driving into her pussy even as it convulsed in ecstasy. His orgasm was hot on the heels of hers, and the kiss that he gave her was the tenderest and most intimate she had known for years. Jacques' orgasm started as the lift passed the fourth floor, and by the time it had reached the eighth both their orgasms were subsiding and he was pulling out of her, his dick still jerking and spilling aftershocks of spunk on the floor of the lift. A tiny jet of liquid squirted across the lift in an arc and splashed the inside of Alice's thigh.

Alice bowed her head: she had no strength left to fight whatever Jacques had in store for her now. Would he leave her here, bound and hanging, her pink pussy dripping with his cum? She wouldn't put it past him. He put his fist in her mouth, and she wondered what he was doing for a second, until he ripped off the vibrator that he had taped to her clit. She understood then that his hand in her mouth was to stifle the scream of pain as he removed the tiny strip of pubic hair that remained on her pussy. His total denuding of her mound was his final way of showing her who was in control here.

'Please let me go.'

'For once I think you've earned it,' he said and, using the scissors again, he snipped at the black tape that bound her at the ankles. Alice hung by her wrists for an agonising moment, until Jacques severed those bonds and caught her when she fell, her tortured body subject to uncontrollable tremors. Gently, with a tenderness that was at odds with the brutal treatment that he had just subjected her to, he placed her down on the floor where she lay, shaking and helpless.

'Is it over now?' Jacques didn't answer. Instead, he turned his back to her, pressed the button for Alice's landing and gathered up his scissors, the toy and the tattered bundle of cloth which had only minutes ago been a designer dress.

When they got to the fourth floor, Jacques opened the lift and watched as Alice grabbed her handbag and staggered to her front door. She could hear voices echoing up the marble staircase, and recognised them as the neighbours who shared her landing. They were complaining about the lift, assuming it was broken. She could make out every word they said, and knew that she probably only had seconds to spare before they saw her, naked but for bracelets and ankle chains made of thick black tape, a red raw imprint of the lift shaft like a waffle pattern on her backside and sore, nude, red flesh where the tape had ripped off her bush. Somehow she managed to get through the door just in time for them to come around and hear it slam. Running was difficult, because her pussy was still so swollen, but Alice managed to dash across her apartment, tender breasts feeling every tiny jiggle, and with Jacques' spunk running down the inside of her legs, to the bedroom where she looked in vain for a sign of Jacques leaving the building.

She stood there until the light faded and she grew cold, but Jacques did not leave by the front door. Looking down at her black-taped wrists gave her a fresh wave of arousal, and she was reluctant to remove the tape, and not just because it would sting as she ripped out the tiny hairs on her wrists and ankles. That black tape and the tiny bruises and tenderness it left was the only sign she had, the only proof, the only physical evidence that Jacques had ever been there.

CHAPTER TEN

The last of the letters was the most audaciously delivered. Alice found it quite by accident, rolling over in her sleep at night to escape Pierre's chunky, outflung limbs, which seemed to take over the entire bed but never to reach out and entwine with her own any more. Shuffling over to the very edge of the bed and dragging her pillow with her, Alice heard the tell-tale crumpling of paper and, sliding her hand into the pillow case where the sound was emanating from, was astounded to find another envelope, the paper slightly dented and warm. Alice went from half asleep to wide, heart-hammering wakefulness. He had been in her bed! Was he here now? Was he going to wake Pierre? She took a few deep breaths to calm herself. No. Jacques was not here now. She would know. She always knew when he was near: her body told her.

A glance at the bedside clock told her that it was 3:30 a.m., a time of night when no one is awake apart from lovers, which explained why Pierre was comatose and snoring beside her. Alice ran to the bathroom and locked herself in before turning on the light. There was that hand-writing, the looping, artistic script which itself had become an aphrodisiac to her of late. She gazed at her written name for a few seconds, savouring the anticipation.

Tomorrow afternoon, 4 p.m., 222 Rue Nicolas, Clichy Sous-Bois.

The address was unfamiliar to Alice. It was 6 a.m. before she was able to sleep again.

She was at the address at the appointed hour, again with her hair hidden underneath a scarf, but she need not have bothered. Number 222 Rue Nicolas was a tumbledown block of flats in one of run-down banlieux, the sprawling Parisian suburbs that Alice never had occasion to frequent. She stood before the building, waiting for Jacques to find her, aware of her expensive clothes and shoes compared to the shabby tracksuits and cheap jeans of the women who passed her and stared at her.

Suddenly a key dropped at her feet. Alice glanced up and saw a familiar figure leaning out of a window only to dart back in again. She quickly calculated that he was in the second flat on the third-floor balcony, and took the concrete steps two at a time, not pausing to read the graffiti and trying to block her nose to the stale smell of urine that permeated the stairwell. She stood in front of the door where she thought Jacques was and nervously tried the key. It worked first time.

He was standing there in the middle of the room that was little bigger than the studio flat he had occupied in Cannes when they had first met. But this room was elegantly furnished, with seagrass carpeting, an elegant steel kitchen tucked into one corner, a couple of tasteful paintings and a plasma TV set. The studio was dominated by a vast white bed. Jacques wore only a pair of jeans and his feet were bare.

'Join me on the bed,' he said. 'Just come and sit with me.'

Alice did so. It was the first time they had been alone like this since Jacques had come back into her life. No one was watching (as far as she knew), there was no danger of discovery, no threat of being caught, no sex toys, no games. That attractive leer of cruelty had gone from his face. She sat next to him, suddenly feeling as shy and clueless as she had done as a teenager.

Jacques had a remote control in his hand. When he pressed it, the screen opposite the bed flickered into life, and images of the first film Alice had ever starred in began to play. The quality of the film was very poor, because of the quality of light and the age of the tape, but it was beautifully shot. Jacques' filmmaking had perfectly captured the spontaneous, joyful, playful and intensely sexual nature of the amazing thing the four young people, high on lust and life, had shared one summer's evening. Alice was entranced to watch herself writhe and moan in ecstasy on the screen. She had been worried the tape would look like a drunken fumble, or worse, that it would be the kind of gynaecological, overly graphic close-up shots which she found so unappealing about most mainstream pornographic films.

Alice was used to seeing herself on screen, but this was no ordinary performance. She realised that although she had been filmed a million times in her life, she had never actually seen *herself* reflected on screen. She watched as her eighteen-year-old image arched her back and stretched her arms over her head as Jacques, lithe and nimble as an alleycat, slid a perfectly smooth, impressively large cock in between her legs and effortlessly penetrated her. She could remember how it had felt exactly that time, the completeness she had felt when his dick was in her cunt. She tasted his lips on hers, remembered the wine they had shared and the smell of the bedclothes.

Then came the scenes of Alice and Julie: these shots were artistic and beautiful, erotica not pornography, as they captured the moment Alice tasted a woman's body the first time. She was aware of a fluttering in her clitoris and hardening in her nipples as she watched Francis and

Jacques have a mock swordfight with their hard pricks, whacking their rods against each other, laughing in delight as the tips of their cocks touched and something like an electric current passed between their young male bodies. Alice had missed this the first time around as she had been so absorbed in exploring Julie's body. The two men were kneeling on the bed, touching and tugging each other's balls and placing their hands on each other's chests. Seeing the two men like this aroused the voyeur in Alice. She felt herself grow wet.

Ignoring Jacques' number-one rule that she was not allowed to approach him, she leaned over to his side of the bed and kissed him, slowly, deeply and passionately. It reminded her of the first kiss they had ever shared, but this one was tinged with sadness, regret at the way she had treated him, despair at the state of her marriage, anger at the way Jacques had come back into her life and tried to control her: all these feelings mixed into a great big bubble of lust and frustration that needed to be burst. Jacques resisted her kiss at first, allowing his lips to remain passive and his jaw slack while she pressed her face against his, but the hardening dick on his lap as Alice straddled him told a different story. After so long playing games of power and domination, neither of them was in control. Their bodies took over and they began to make love. Alice unfastened her button-down dress; Jacques slid out of his jeans like a snake shedding its skin while Alice slipped out of her panties.

Their nude bodies were pressed together like layers of paper, Jacques on his back with his hard-on pressing in between Alice's legs, Alice face down on top of him, losing track of where her flesh ended and his began. Sliding her body up so that her breasts were on his shoulders and his dick was nestling near her clit, she allowed the tip of his penis to brush her clitoris for a few seconds before lowering herself down on to his erection. His cock was thicker and firmer than she had ever known it, and it filled her up perfectly. Spreading her legs wide, Alice thrust and ground her pussy against Jacques' pubic bone, letting the rasp of his pubic hair tickle and tease her clit, enjoying the extra stretch her cunt received when he pressed his hips up towards hers, forcing his dick even deeper inside her. His hands were on her arse, not spanking or being rough with her, but gently stroking the creamy skin of her buttocks, guiding her hips, tracing a faint line up and down her spine, sending shivers of desire all over her body.

He took her face in his, and she did the same to him, finding that the slow, lazy kiss they exchanged got her wetter and hornier than the urgent, probing kisses she had been used to of late. Jacques thrust upwards once, twice, three times, until she felt she would burst with the bulk of his cock, and her swollen clit would explode with tension. He pulled his tongue away from her lips then pushed his thumb in her mouth to lubricate it and then parted her arse cheeks before stabbing at her anus with the slippery digit, jabbing it inside and twisting his hand around so that every secret area of her was explored and conquered. She surrendered to the hot, liquid orgasm that rippled from her clit to her tits to her fingers and toes. She felt her cheeks and chest grow warm and prickle with heat. Her pussy squeezed his prick and he emptied his balls, jets of spunk pumping into her, his balls slapping against his thighs as he jerked and convulsed.

They lay in silence with Alice's pussy occasionally twitching around Jacques' subsiding hard-on. Jacques wrapped his arms around Alice, and the last words she said before she abandoned the wakeful world for a deep sleep were, 'I'm so sorry I hurt you. I wish I'd never left you. How could I have let this go?'

When Alice woke it was dark outside, and she was alone. The one-bedroom apartment was illuminated by a single floor lamp, and on top of the television was the video-tape they had watched a few hours ago. Alice felt a surge of panic. Where was Jacques? She ran to the tiny bath-room. No Jacques. She flipped the light on. The pile of books that had been on the bedside table were gone.

Feeling sick, Alice pulled open the wardrobe. The space inside was empty apart from a few jangling wire coathangers and a small blue envelope. Stifling a scream, Alice tore it open and read the message inside.

Now it's over.

She understood. He had given her the tape, removed the threat to her career. She was safe and need not fear his games any more. But the last game he had played had been the cruellest of all and he had finally got his revenge on her. He had made her fall in love with him. And then he had gone. She knew that however long she waited at that apartment, he would not come back. There would be no more letters.

Alice placed her hand between her legs, rubbed her pussy and sniffed her fingers, as though inhaling the vanishing traces of their last fuck would preserve the feeling and the memory. She placed her fingertip on the tip of her tongue and tasted the tang of his spunk for the last time. Naked and alone in a bare apartment in a strange district, Alice Daumier, the cool, composed actress, threw herself on the floor and howled.

CHAPTER ELEVEN

The latest film directed by Pierre Daumier and starring his wife Alice was being premiered at the Cannes film festival. These days, Alice always travelled to Cannes by air. Often, Pierre had suggested they take the train for old times' sake but that would have awoken the memories that Alice had tried so hard to suppress. It had been years since he had suggested the train. Now it was a given that they would travel in a private jet and this year was no exception.

Just one month ago, Alice would have adored the luxury of the private jet, the champagne, the masseuse, the glittering showbiz gossip that could be exchanged on board. The plane's human cargo was precious: the passengers included Alice, Pierre, Delphine, a stylist and make-up artist and Duke Levante, the handsome co-star of the film. Tall, black and extremely flirtatious, he teased Alice in his deep Southern American drawl about the questions the press would ask about their on-screen chemistry.

'So, ma'am,' he said, turning his career-defining smile

on Alice. 'You happy to talk about all the hot sex we been havin'?'

The sex scene they had filmed – Alice's first in mainstream cinema – was a saccharine, Hollywood cliché but it was the first time Alice had ever done a nude scene for Pierre and press speculation was rife. Alice thought back to the early days when Pierre had promised that he would establish her as a serious dramatic actress. Now he was directing romantic comedies that made the couple materially rich but left her feeling hollow and unsatisfied.

'Oh yes,' said Alice, laughing. 'Our torrid affair.' There had been chemistry, but she had forced herself not to get turned on by Duke's hard muscle which contrasted so beautifully with the softness of his skin, the squareness of his jaw, and the tenderness of his lips. Ever the dutiful wife, Alice had not allowed herself to become aroused. Of course, that had been before Jacques had come back into her life and reawakened her. Before he had abandoned her.

Alice had long been nursing a suspicion that Duke was not the red-blooded, heterosexual action man that his movie career portrayed him to be. Throughout the whole time they were filming, he had turned down offers from stunning actresses, extras, make-up girls and fans. Few women could resist flirting with Duke, and while he was always happy to indulge in highly flirtatious banter, he had never to Alice's knowledge taken things further with any woman.

When the plane touched down at the airport, the party were ferried to the hotel in separate cars. Delphine dashed to meet journalists, Duke had his own car, and Alice found herself alone in the back of a chauffeur-driven limousine with Pierre. She wondered if she was being paranoid, as she felt that Pierre was once more radiating a silent disapproval in her direction. Her fears were proved right when he told her what to wear for that night's press conference, and later premiere.

'We need to make sure you project the right image, Alice,' he said. 'Lately, there has been something strange about you. I don't know what it is, and I hope you'll snap out of it, but our marriage is a brand and we have to present it to the world as such. You're here as my wife first, star of your own film second. Do you understand?'

Alice reeled from Pierre's harsh, controlling words and the chilly tone in which he spoke them. Once he had wanted her to be his muse. Now he only saw her as another business proposition. Alice felt resentful. How dare he try to control her? To dictate the very clothes she wore? Only one man had ever earned the right to tell her what to do, and that was not her husband.

The hotel suite was vast. Alice claimed the main bedroom as her own, telling Pierre she would need a separate space to dress in. He didn't demur at the prospect of spending the night in separate beds. Alone in her room, Alice looked out on her balcony that overlooked the seafront. It was already swarming with press, yachts bobbing on the horizon, red carpets and marquees springing up on every patch of green space. She heard the chink of ice in a glass to her right, and realised that her balcony almost immediately gave on to Duke's. He was drinking vodka on the rocks and was shirtless. His ebony skin glistened in the early evening sunlight.

They exchanged pleasantries about the interviews they were scheduled to do that afternoon and moaned about how intrusive it was when the press asked about your private life. I wonder what you've got to hide, thought Alice, looking slyly at Duke. I worked with you every day but you're still a mystery to me. She could recognise a man with something to hide. They had that in common.

Alice gave her interviews on autopilot, switching between English and French and saying nothing of real interest in either language. She was well versed in giving up the same standard reply to all questions and it wasn't as if the journalists were ever after anything original anyway. Effortlessly she deflected any questions about her and Duke by praising his acting skills and ignoring sexual innuendo. She was relieved when the interviews were over and it was time to dress for the premiere. The dress her stylist had selected was a 1980s vintage Valentino gown, a backless blue dress which scooped in her boyish figure and gave her curves in all the right places. Her make-up artist piled her hair up in a loose, messy chignon with a couple of strands tumbling down to frame her face. Alice's eyes were ringed with navy kohl and royal blue eyeshadow, and false eyelashes made her eyes look huge. Alice looked dirty, rocky, edgy, far from the wholesome image Pierre wanted her to project, but she was sick of by-the-book elegance and wanted to make her own mark on the festival.

She and Pierre walked the red carpet in silence, professional smiles fixed to their faces. Flashbulbs dazzled Alice and fans and paparazzi screamed her name. Even with the lenses of the world's press trained on her, she still didn't feel *watched* as she had done when Jacques was there. She would know if he was watching her. And she didn't feel it. Couldn't smell him on the sea air. Didn't feel the hairs on the back of her neck rise and her nipples stiffen.

The second they entered the marquee, Pierre dropped Alice's arm and ingratiated himself with a circle of Hollywood executives in black ties. Alice found herself hanging out with Duke and his companion Maurizio Villeneuve, a young French male model who was trying to make the transition between the billboard and the big screen. Maurizio was good-looking in an angular, feline sort of way, with a deep tan and cropped blond hair. He also had a filthy sense of humour and a bitchy aside for every other guest at the party. Alice found herself laughing in a way that she had not done for longer than she could remember. Not just since Jacques had come back, but also, perhaps, the years before that. At midnight, the music got louder and the guests younger and sillier.

'I've had enough of this place,' said Duke, reading her thoughts. 'We might as well continue the party back at my hotel room. You two are the only ones worth talking to in this room anyway.'

So, with a devastatingly handsome man on each arm, Alice Daumier strode back down the red carpet, winking at the paparazzi. She knew that the image of her flanked by such fine specimens would ensure front-page coverage for the film the next day.

Back in Duke's hotel room, they drank cocktails on the balcony. Alice kicked off her shoes, suddenly aware of how tiny she was next to the huge men.

'The lights and the glamour are so much better when you're far away from them,' she said, as they watched yachts bobbing in the harbour and listened to the sound of parties drift up from the street.

'I'd rather be up here with you two, anyway,' said Maurizio. 'It's rather exciting hanging out with the couple from the poster.' There was something suggestive in the way that he spoke, and Alice realised that he was flirting with both of them. Duke's voice took on a deeper and more serious tone when he replied.

'We're a very attractive threesome,' he said.

The word 'threesome' sent a sexual charge through Alice and she suddenly had a vision of these two men satisfying her body at the same time. She felt the familiar heat begin to grow between her legs. Her nipples began to harden and a blush crept up her neck and cheeks. And was it her imagination, or were Maurizio and Duke moving closer in towards her? She was pressed on one side by lithe, lightly tanned flesh and felt Duke's chiselled bulk on the other. They moved in closer and closer until Alice could hear both their heartbeats and feel their pulses hammering. This was definitely not her imagination. She let out a whimper of excitement as the men, towering above her, began to kiss, their bodies drawing even closer and crushing Alice's fragile frame. As two erections pressed into her flesh at waist height, Alice felt that she would suffocate between their bodies, and contemplated with a smile that it wouldn't be a bad way to go.

The men pulled apart just before Alice fainted and turned their attention from each other to her. Duke's hands travelled down Alice's bare back and then slid underneath the fabric of her dress to caress her ribs and stomach but tantalisingly avoided her tingling breasts. Maurizio bent down and kissed Alice on the mouth, slowly and tenderly. Alice reached one hand out towards Maurizio's crotch and the other behind her and felt for Duke's dick. Both men were big and hard. She began to rub her hands up and down the bulges in the men's trousers, a leisurely motion at first, but then increasing in size and speed. Duke bent down and nibbled the top of Alice's ear. His breath on her sensitive skin was warm and sweet. Maurizio's tongue continued to explore Alice's mouth while Duke's large hands finally made their way to her breasts and massaged the soft flesh and hard nipples. All three of them began to moan in unison, Duke's voice soft in Alice's ear, Alice and Maurizio groaning through their kiss. Alice rubbed their dicks harder and faster, astonished that the men were still getting bigger and harder, fumbling with their buckles, eager to unleash the two pricks.

The three bodies began to undress each other in movements so deft, slow and tender that they might have been choreographed. Alice raised her hands up over her head and Maurizio and Duke both gathered the shiny blue fabric of her dress and lifted it over her head. Alice pulled at the buttons of Maurizio's shirt as Duke slid his fingers around the waistband of her panties, stroked her through the damp cotton of her gusset and slid them all the way down her legs, his fingers tickling and teasing her inner thighs, the backs of her knees, and finally her ankles. Alice kicked the panties off, grateful to have the fresh air on her throbbing pussy, standing there with her legs slightly parted. Alice took a step back and watched the men undress each other, all the better to savour the moment when their cocks were unveiled for the first time. Duke and Maurizio tore at each other's clothes with an aggression that Alice found overpoweringly masculine and thrilling. Duke grabbed Maurizio's hips, unzipped the other man's fly and forced the black trousers down over a pair of snake-like hips. A long, thick hard-on popped up from underneath a dark-blond bush. Maurizio reciprocated, sliding his hand inside Duke's trousers and holding on to the erection inside before allowing the trousers to fall to the floor. Duke was bigger and thicker even than Maurizio. Alice's clit was calling her, and her fingers found their way between her legs. She began to stroke the swollen nub of flesh, wondering if the men would fuck in front of her while she watched, or if they would take it in turns to penetrate her, or if she would take both dicks in her mouth. Her eyes kept darting between Duke's chunky ebony body and Maurizio's younger, slimmer, tawny one as the two men embraced face to face and shared a deep, lingering kiss. As one, they reached out to pull Alice towards them and she was back where she had started, her body pressed between theirs, their now-naked flesh providing an overwhelming sensation. Alice felt Duke's dick jab at the small of her back while Maurizio's prodded her belly button, her arse squashed against the solidity of Duke's thighs while her tits rubbed against the light down on Maurizio's chest.

Turning her body so that she was looking out over the sea, Alice stood on the balcony, a prick in each hand, feeling powerful and alive. She knew just what she wanted to do. She knelt down on the floor, opened her mouth and closed her eyes. She parted her legs, exposing the dark rose of her cunt with its coating of musky liquid, waiting to welcome whoever wanted to fuck her. She kept her eyes screwed shut, not wanting to know which man was in her mouth and which was in her pussy, but as a thick dick prodded at her lips, she felt the soft wiry hair of a white man's bush and knew that it was Maurizio who would be fucking her in the face. His balls slapped on her chin as she greedily let her throat fall open to accommodate the long, smooth dick. She tasted pre-cum and drank it greedily down.

Shuffling sounds and a warm presence behind her told Alice that Duke was getting ready to penetrate her yearning pussy. Her legs began to shake as the first probings of her vulva told her that this hard-on was as big as Alice had ever had, and then a little bigger. Duke seemed to understand, and eased his prick in slowly, using the tip of his penis to massage Alice's G-spot, before building up to stronger, more rhythmic thrusts that tested the capacity of Alice's cunt to its limit. Her natural lubrication helped her to accommodate the huge log as it drove into her hole, more merciless with every stroke. Alice screamed, her cries muffled by Maurizio's thrusting cock and intensifying the sensation for him. She reached forward and began to rub her clit again, using her free hand to grab on to Maurizio's leg. She opened her eyes, looked up at the perfect face and the model's body which had made him famous. But few had seen him like this, his perfect features contorted with the effort it was obviously taking him not to come. And then there was that tanned, flat stomach with its faint line of hair like an arrow pointing from the navel to the dick. Just as Alice was savouring this visual treat, Duke began to thrust harder and faster than before, forcing her whole body to topple forward. Alice found that the force of Duke's thrusts were shoving her body hard up against Maurizio, so that his dick was deeper in her throat than any, even Jacques', had been before. The feeling of a man in each end of Alice's body gave her a sense of completeness and fullness that she loved. She rubbed her clit as fast as her swaying, out-of-control body would allow, and her whole pussy began to flutter deliciously, always a sign she was mere seconds away from orgasm.

Maurizio came first, as Alice knew he would. She felt

his balls rise up into his body and saw the muscles at the sides of his arse and thighs tense up seconds before he pulled out of her. His orgasm delivered a jet of white milky liquid that did not hit her face but spilled out over her back and decorated Duke's chin and chest. Duke was next, his climax forcing his dick so deep inside Alice she felt her internal organs squashed and she laughed with pleasure. Duke too pulled out the moment he had come, splashing his seed over her back and arse. Alice was left naked and on all fours, skin covered in the mixed-up spunk of two men but without the orgasm she craved. Brazenly, she rolled on to her back and spread her legs, her protruding and frustrated clitoris a challenge to either man to satisfy her. Both obliged by dropping to their knees. Maurizio took Alice's right breast in his mouth and swirled his tongue over the hard little nipple, while Duke delved between her legs and flickered his tongue over Alice's aching clit. Two men and two mouths finally achieved the release of tension that two dicks had not and Alice surrendered to an over-powering orgasm, feeling her convulsing cunt twitch and flutter in the balmy night air.

The three of them spent the rest of the evening drinking naked on the balcony, laughing at the paparazzi just a few metres below them. Alice slipped back into her dress and tiptoed back into her suite at first light. The final image she saw as she closed Duke's door behind her was of the two men reaching for each other. She showered and got into bed, relishing the experience she'd just had and trying to ignore the feeling that all she really wanted now was for Jacques to hold her while she went to sleep.

CHAPTER TWELVE

After Cannes, Alice slumped into a deep depression. She and Pierre were living completely separate lives, and when he flew to Hollywood for talks with a producer he'd met at the festival, he didn't bother to kiss her goodbye. She was alone. No Jacques, no work, no husband, with only a grainy, eight-year-old videotape for company. She didn't even own a video recorder any more – and she wasn't sure she could have borne to watch the tape even if she had. It would be too intense a reminder of what she had thrown away. Alice didn't wash, didn't answer the phone, drank wine instead of eating and didn't leave the house for ten days.

On the eleventh morning, something inside Alice changed. She woke early, shrugged off the mantle of self-pity and became steely and determined. She called Delphine, who sounded relieved and angry and told her that she had been so worried by Alice's silence that she was on the verge of coming to her apartment and breaking the door down. Alice told Delphine that she would be in the office for a meeting at 9 a.m. – two hours' time. Alice showered and washed her hair, feeling positive and confident.

Delphine remained silent throughout the meeting as Alice told her everything. Her eyes grew wider and occasionally she let out a little laugh of disbelief.

'I can't believe you, Alice,' says Delphine. 'You had a secret past and a secret lover that I never knew about. I thought we told each other everything!' Then she switched from friend mode into agent mode, brisk and businesslike and looking for a solution. 'So. What are we going to do now?'

Alice sketched the outlines of the plan she had made.

'No,' said Delphine firmly. 'No fucking way. It'd be career suicide.'

'What career?' wailed Alice. 'Starring in another one of Pierre's crappy romantic comedies? None of this is the real me. With Jacques I can be true to myself. Sex with him is the only time I feel truly alive. I'll go back to doing theatre work, I'll start at the bottom again, doing the work I want to. Jacques would have understood that it isn't about fame or money.'

'I think you're a crazy lady,' said Delphine. 'But you've convinced me. Let's do it.' Alice opened her Birkin bag and handed the tape over to Delphine, who examined it as though it were a bomb about to explode, then sighed and flicked through her contacts book. She made a call to her technological advisor, Laurent, and once she had confirmed that it would be easy for him to transfer an old videotape on to a disc, summoned him to the office. He was there in half an hour.

'OK,' Delphine instructed Laurent. 'There's a huge bonus for you if you sign this confidentiality agreement before you start.' Once Laurent had signed, Delphine handed the cassette to him and said, 'Edit this down to half an hour.'

Delphine watched slack-jawed and amazed at the footage that Laurent worked with, and poor Laurent crouched awkwardly over his computer screen in a vain attempt to conceal his hard-on.

'Can you edit it so that the other people's faces aren't visible?' asked Alice, thinking of Julie and Francis. 'So that it's just me and Jacques you see?'

Laurent nodded, and showed her how he could zoom in close so that while the dick play between Francis and Jacques was visible, their faces were not. Alice nodded her approval.

'Christ, Alice,' Delphine sighed in a breathy, low voice that betrayed her arousal. 'This is hot stuff. Are you sure you want us to do this?' Alice nodded, unable to speak, fixated on the moving image of Jacques' cock, the column of flesh sliding in and out of her pussy. She crossed her legs and squeezed her thighs together to give some small gratification to her swelling clit.

By noon that day, an edited version of the film, with Julie's and Francis's identities obscured, had been posted on the internet. By 12.30 every journalist in Paris had called Delphine demanding to know if it was really Alice. Delphine played the game for a while, pretending she didn't know anything about it, and insisting that she was sure her client had never taken part in a pornographic film. The ploy worked: the story made the front page of every newspaper in France, all the British tabloids, and gossip magazines in the USA and Australia. Headlines speculated on Alice's identity with undisguised relish. Even the serious-minded broadsheets covered the tape, praising it as a beautifully shot, tender and sensitive piece of film-making.

Pierre got his secretary to call Delphine, saying that he was suing Alice for divorce.

'Best news I've heard for ages,' said Delphine to Alice, who felt only relief.

After two days of frenzied press speculation, Delphine issued a statement saying that she could confirm that the images on the film did indeed portray an eighteen-year-old Alice Daumier, or Alice Hill as she was then known. Her statement was curt but to the point. 'My client made the film when she was a drama student and it was prior to her relationship with Pierre Daumier. I am also saddened to announce that Monsieur Daumier has asked for the marriage to be dissolved with immediate effect.'

Now it had been confirmed that it was indeed Alice in the footage, speculation about the others' identity grew. Journalists assumed that it must be one of the other three participants who had leaked the tape – it did not occur to anyone that Alice Daumier would sabotage her own career in this way. Julie and Francis they could not hope to identify, but Jacques' face, frozen in orgasm, was plastered over front pages under the banner: 'Who's That Guy?'

Alice waited for him to give her a sign that he was watching her but none came. She braced herself for somebody from her past – distant or recent – to contribute to the story. But neither Julie nor Francis came forward and to Alice's gratification, Sylvie was true to her word and maintained a dignified silence. She had never expected Jacques to sell his story. But she knew that he would know that all this was a plea for him to get back in touch with her. She had taken a gamble and she had been so sure it would pay off. As the days passed, Alice had to confront the terrible possibility that she had exposed herself and ruined her career and marriage and that Jacques still wasn't going to come for her.

Alice moved into a hotel on the Rive Gauche which

she and Delphine made into a miniature office. It was the only place she could get the privacy she craved. They spent hours poring over the various offers of interviews from television and print. They decided that they would have much more impact if she made a live announcement on television, to tell everybody exactly what had been going on. After all, in print, journalists can twist your words and put their own meaning and spin on to things. On camera, especially when the broadcast is live, there is no room to hide and no possibility for manipulation.

Alice decided to give her only TV interview to Sandrine Boucher, a formidable talk-show host in her late forties whose evening programme invariably dominated the ratings. Alice rose on the morning of the interview feeling like Marie Antoinette about to go to the guillotine. And, like that French queen, she dressed to impress for her execution. She decided to play up to her new image as a scarlet woman and wore a red wrap dress that clung like a second skin around her waist, but flared out around her hips, the hemline resting demurely just below her knee. Her hair was piled up on top of her head, and held in place with a single chopstick, a little tribute to Julie, who she hoped would be watching, somewhere.

As the theme tune played, Alice walked down the steps to the sofa where the interview was going to take place. To her delight, the audience gave her a standing ovation. The lights of the studio were blazing hot, and Alice basked in their comforting heat. Sandrine had no script and began with one single question.

'Welcome, Alice. Now, will you please tell us what is going on?'

And Alice talked, feeling a surge of euphoric relief as she unburdened herself of the secrets she had been carrying around for her whole adult life. She started her story where it had begun, as a naïve eighteen-year-old leaving London for a new life in France, going on to describe her first meeting with Jacques, her sexual awakening, her regret at leaving him. She did not tell Sandrine about her more recent adventures, the games and the punishments and the torches and the sweet surrenders that had made her feel more alive than at any time since she had first met Jacques. Those were not for sharing, not with the nation, not with anyone but Jacques.

'I was crazy to leave,' she said. 'I know now that what Jacques and I had was so rare that if you find it, you don't throw it away. What can I say? I was eighteen, ambitious, I thought that career and love were incompatible. I have since realised that all the money and fame in the world is worthless if you betray yourself and your body on such a fundamental level.'

'And who do you think leaked the tape?' demanded Sandrine. Alice looked at her lap, hoping to look demure and innocent and also because she could not hide the smile that played about her lips.

'It could have been any one of them, I really couldn't say. I don't know why they have chosen this moment to expose me like this. But I suppose they have done me a favour. Now the public gets to see the real me. And hopefully, I will have made some of my fans very, very happy indeed.'

A ripple of laughter waved through the audience. Alice laughed with them, and Sandrine had to repeat her next question.

'Alice,' she pressed. 'Alice, where is Jacques now?'

Alice turned to the camera. It was time to give the speech that she had rehearsed in her head. 'I don't know. If he was near me, I would know, because his body would call mine, and I would respond. I could not help but respond. I have faith that he is watching me now, and I know that we will be together soon.'

'We will end on that intriguing note,' said Sandrine. 'Alice Daumier, thank you for sharing your story with us tonight. I think we can all agree that whatever happens, life will change very much for you in the future. I for one think you are a fabulous, sexy, creative woman who has been stifled by her own ambition, by a shallow industry and by the wrong marriage. I hope that you find your wild horse, and that the pair of you run free together.'

Alice was incredibly touched by Sandrine's words, and fought back tears. She was grateful when the studio lights dimmed and the theme music blared out of the studio speakers. Removing her microphone from her lapel, Sandrine leaned forward and whispered into Alice's ear, 'And if you ever fancy another Sapphic adventure, do call me. I'd love to eat your pussy.' Alice gave a surprised, flattered giggle. And as she took off her own microphone, and made her way backstage to where Delphine waited, the adrenaline rush of being on live television and the suggestive thrill that Sandrine's words had sent through her made her feel invigorated, alive, gave her a hint of the feeling she had missed.

Delphine was in the green room, her mobile phone attached to her ear, but she flipped it shut when she saw Alice approaching.

'The phones are going wild,' she said, kissing Alice on both cheeks. 'Your gamble paid off. Everybody loves you. The phone is ringing with offers of work. Far from destroying your career, I think you have just gone from star to superstar.'

'But did *he* call?' Alice asked, urgently. Delphine shook her head sadly. Alice shrugged. The hope she had hardly dared to nurture had been dashed.

A security guard approached Delphine and had a hushed conversation with her.

'There are too many paparazzi outside,' said Delphine. 'I think we'll take you out of the back way, because otherwise it's just gonna get crazy. I want you to have all this attention, but I don't want you to get hurt. And besides,' she said with a smile, 'it never does any harm to always leave them wanting a little more of you.'

'That's fine by me,' said Alice, who did not want to emerge from her triumphant interview with her face crumpled with disappointment that Jacques had not been in touch.

The security guard led them through a warren of corridors in the TV studio, bare breeze-blocked walls that seemed to go on for ever and twisted and turned until it was impossible to retain any sense of direction. The security guard stopped and pointed them towards a fire exit at the end of the long corridor and told them they would be able to make their way into a back street which would be free from photographers.

'Which street?' Delphine asked the guard. 'I need to tell the car to come and pick us up.' He gave her an address and Delphine flipped open her phone to notify the driver of the change of plan. 'Damn,' said Delphine. 'I can't get a signal. Wait here, Alice, I'll meet you back down there by the fire escape once I've spoken to the driver.'

Alice nodded, grateful to have the chance to be alone at last. She closed her eyes, inhaled and exhaled slowly.

Her breath echoed along the corridor's bare walls. Idly, slowly, Alice walked down the end of the corridor towards the door. When she saw something on the floor, in the distance, something that may or may not have been a small, square, pale blue slip of paper, she caught her breath and dared not hope. She sprinted in her heels and bent down to read.

Look behind you

She was afraid to look. But she knew he was there; as she had told Sandrine, he was calling her body with his, a wordless command that had to be obeyed. She turned around to find him just an inch behind her so that his lips were almost level with hers. There was no need for them to speak. Alice's breath began to come in short rasps and her nipples stiffened, as she closed her eyes and opened her mouth, allowed his tongue to fly between her lips and kiss her aggressively. His turgid prick was out of his trousers and in her hand within a matter of seconds. She slid her hand up and down its shaft, marvelling again at its peachy flesh. Not bothering to remove her panties, she pulled them to one side. The pulse in her pussy pounded in time to her heartbeat, fast and urgent and rhythmic. She didn't wait to get wet but spread her legs and the fat cock that parted her pussy lips drove into her and tore at her flesh, a sharp burst of pain followed by the pleasure and comfort that only Jacques' dick inside her could bring.

'God, you're tight,' he said, turning his hips so that his cock twisted inside her, massaging her pussy walls. He pulled down her dress and exposed her breasts, pert and pointy with hard nipples. 'Tight and dry as a virgin.'

She didn't stay dry for long. The lace of her panties chafed at her clit, flooding her cunt with liquid. Jacques lifted her hips up so that she was impaled on his cock, legs dangling helplessly down by her sides. She banged her head on the wall as he staggered forward. She didn't care. She bashed her elbow and grazed it on the rough unpainted walls of the corridor. She didn't care. Delphine, the security guard, any random member of staff could have witnessed their animal union. She didn't care. And she began half-talking, half-sobbing with his tongue in her mouth.

'Fuck me, Jacques, you dirty bastard,' she breathed. 'Fuck me and fuck me and fuck me for ever.'

Her hungry cunt devoured his dick. She reached her hand in between her legs and tugged at his balls and made him cry out, giving as good as she got. He bent his head to her breasts, bit the nipples so hard he almost drew blood, and then tenderly sucked them and soothed them. She made her fingers into a claw and scratched her name into the small of his back.

'You horny slut,' he said through his kiss. 'You need this.'

'Do it to me,' she begged. 'Make me come. Let me come.'

He obliged, sliding his finger in between their pressed bodies, using the back of his knuckle to knead her clit, his wrist flexing fast and furiously, putting just the right pressure on the engorged nub of flesh, making her whole body weak. He came first, the low growl that emanated from his body awakening something primal in her, and she let out a wild animal howl, desperate for her own orgasm. His prick was still twitching and oozing post-cum droplets when he bent down on his knees, knelt between her legs and sucked out his own spunk, his tongue darting in and out of her ravenous cunt like a miniature dick before flickering lightly over her clit, his breath warm on her flesh. When she came, a hot, pounding orgasm, her juices gushed over his face. The kiss that came next was salty and tender. They said it at the same time, whispered it while their mouths were full of each other's smells and tastes.

'I love you.'

They pulled apart, Alice using her panties to mop up her swollen cunt, Jacques tucking his spent penis back inside his trousers, and they exchanged a look that said more than words ever could. We've done it, the look said, we're finally equal, you have played me at my own game and won, and from today everything will be different.

Without speaking they joined hands, opened the fire-escape door and ran out into the alleyway into a rainy evening, the cool, dirty water soothing their skin which was still hot from their sex, jumping into the car that had just pulled up with an open-mouthed Delphine in the passenger seat behind the driver. 'Go!' Alice shouted to the man behind the wheel, and she and Jacques ducked down in the back seat and the wheels covered the waiting paparazzi in a splash of grey Parisian puddle water.

Back at the hotel, Delphine was still coming to terms with meeting Jacques in such extraordinary circumstances.

'It was a PR masterstroke,' she said. 'I couldn't have planned it better myself. They think you're Bonnie and Clyde. They can't get enough of you. Anyway, if you two can stop sucking each other's faces long enough to talk business, Alice, I've got lots of offers for you here and we need some answers soon.'

Delphine rattled through a list of unappealing film and TV roles and some intriguing but badly paid theatre work.

'If only you could come back with a really amazing film,' said Delphine.

'I've got an idea,' said Jacques. And he proceeded to

outline the script he'd been working on for the past few years, a beautiful, epic, daring and challenging film about sex during the French Revolution that had the two women captivated and spellbound. The action was seen through the eyes of an upper-class woman who joined the fight for equality and discovered sexual as well as political liberation, joining forces with a feisty working-class female revolutionary. It was the part Alice was born to play.

'We should do it!' said Alice. 'Delphine – it sounds amazing. Can you put some calls in?'

'Leave it with me,' said Delphine. 'I'll be fighting off offers from producers wanting to fund your project. You guys are hot property.' Then, as Alice and Jacques locked lips in a celebratory kiss, 'I'll leave you two here to talk it over.'

'What now?' said Jacques, sliding his hands underneath Alice's top and enjoying the way her nipples turned into tiny pebbles at his touch.

'I think we should begin the casting immediately,' said Alice, as clearly as she could with her lower lip clamped between Jacques' teeth.

'Well, in the immediate future I was planning on bending you over and fucking your tight little pink arsehole,' replied Jacques. 'Not auditioning people.'

'I have a better idea. I think we can combine the two.'

Jacques looked confused as Alice pulled away from him and reached for her telephone.

'Hello, Sylvie,' she purred to the person on the other end of the line. 'It's Alice Daumier here. How are you? Are you still looking for acting projects? I'm making a new film with Jacques – yes, that's him, the guy you met – and we're looking for talent to come and audition for us. Now? Now would be great.' Alice gave Sylvie the address of the hotel and slid her hand into her panties in anticipation of the girl's visit. 'Come soon, Sylvie. I know *we* will.'

True Passion:
A Tale of Desire as Told
to Madame B

Bold sexual adventurer Katie reveals her innermost secrets to our mysterious hostess, Madame B, and tells a tale of seduction and fantasies made real. She falls for the charms of older man Alex, and makes it her mission (and his) to experience every thrill life has to offer.

As Katie pushes their passion to extremes, will Alex surrender to her every whim? *True Passion* tells their scintillating story, and ensures that nothing remains a secret any more.

ISBN: 9780091924881

£6.99

Available now at www.rbooks.co.uk

Too Hot to Handle:
More True Stories
from Madame B

Our mysterious hostess Madame B tells the tales of ten young women who have pushed passion to the very limit. Delicious desires and sexy secrets are revealed, with steamy scenarios and extreme indulgences stripped bare.

Includes:

Executive Decision – It's the career chance of a lifetime. PA to a gorgeous, jet-setting executive. Amanda wants the job – and him – so badly. Then he asks if she has any 'extra services' to offer.

Coming Up Roses – Kara can't face a day in the office and calls in sick. That's when she notices two gardeners working outside. It's hot, they're sweating. So Kara invites them both in for a shower . . .

Double Fantasy – Identical twins Gilly and Annie secretly share their men. So when fit delivery guy Rob turns up with a washing machine, Gilly has her fun on top of it – and then lets Annie take over.

Tunnel Vision – She spots him at check-in, and he's sitting opposite her in first class. He passes her a mobile number. She texts. He texts. And things get steamy.

Backstage Pass – Everyone knows him, the rock star who regularly tops the charts. Ali just has to have him, and blags a backstage pass . . .

ISBN: 9780091924966
£6.99

Available now at www.rbooks.co.uk

Lost in Lust:
More Tales
from Madame B

Madame B is back, with ten more sexy tales from women who do the things you secretly want to do – but would never dare.

Includes:

Hire Love – Hannah hires a male escort for a high-powered work party, but it turns into more than a simple business transaction.

The Mistress's Apprentice – Tina discovers how thrilling power can be when she finds herself working in a place where submission and domination are all in a day's work.

The Hitcher – Alice and Paul's erotic encounter with a young hitchhiker turns into the ride of a lifetime.

Window Shopping – a shared fantasy of sex in public is made real when Bethany and Max take a big risk . . .

El Ritmo del Noche – at a fiesta on holiday in Spain, Helen finds out that even the prissiest English girl needs a little Latin in her.

ISBN: 9780091916480

£6.99

Available now at www.rbooks.co.uk